MANHATTAN GOTHIC

VIVISPHERE
PUBLISHING

Arrighi, Mel.
 Manhattan Gothic
1. Title

ISBN 1-89-2323-80-X
Library of Congress Catalogue Number 99-60521

First Vivisphere Edition

For information: Vivisphere Publishing
                     2 Neptune Road
                     Poughkeepsie, NY 12601

www.vivisphere.com

VIVISPHERE
PUBLISHING

Vivisphere Titles also by Mel Arrighi

The Death Collection (1975)
Daddy Pig (1974)
An Ordinary Man (1970)

MANHATTAN GOTHIC

MEL ARRIGHI

PART ONE

She was a story, at first. A woman, too of course, as beautiful a one as I had seen in a long time. But I had my priorities, and I needed a book idea, not a love affair.

Actually, that night I hadn't expected to find either. Eve Lukas had invited me to come by late, to be, I suspected, a shot-in-the-arm to a dinner party in its dying gasps. She hadn't put it that way, but I was familiar with Eve's strategies.

I arrived at eleven. When I stopped in the entrance hall and glanced into the living room at the guests sitting over their snifters of brandy, I saw, for the most part, faces that were familiar, but familiar to me only from previous evenings there. I felt a slight sinking feeling; this wasn't the most upbeat crowd around.

They were Eve's oldest friends and, life being what it was, most of them had experienced recent bad fortune. The radical professor had lost his chair, the South American diplomat his government, the painter his dealer, the interior decorator her marriage, and they bore the marks of these losses, creased into their faces. As a group, they managed to be cheerful enough, but their brightness was like that of the Abstract Expressionist canvases which, along with Eve's photographs, adorned the walls. It was the leftover brightness of vanished, irreclaimable excitement.

So it was only natural that my gaze went directly to the one young, unlined face in the living room—though it would have caught my attention anywhere. It wasn't a New York face, an American face, or even a twentieth-century face. It was the countenance of a dream-drugged maiden in a pre-Raphaelite painting, framed in thick coils of chestnut hair, the skin pale and porcelain smooth, the large eyes dark and haunted. Those eyes were fixed on me now with peculiar intensity.

I smiled tentatively across the distance, but was soon distracted as Eve came and greeted me with a kiss. At Eve's place, coats went into the bedroom, and that was where I headed. Eve followed me in and closed the door partway behind her. I laid my coat on the bed and then turned to her, wondering what she was up to. A bit of flirtation? I wouldn't have objected. Eve was a fine-looking woman, and the passage of time had not diminished her sensuality. Her curly hair, I noticed, was tinted a bolder red, and the hostess gown she was wearing had a transparency that revealed, with unabashed preciseness, the outline of her curvaceous body.

But Eve, it turned out, simply wanted to pass on a piece of information to me. "The Contessa wants to meet you," she said.

"The Contessa?" I echoed in a puzzled tone, even though I was sure this had to be that beautiful, unearthly young woman.

"Mirella," she said. "Mirella Ludovisi."

"Oh." If Eve hadn't invoked the title first—an odd bit of snobbery in someone who had once considered herself a Trotskyite—I would have realized who the young woman was at once. I knew of her; as a name, anyway, a figure in a tragic occurrence that had taken place some months back.

"You mean, the girl…with Tobias Walling?"

"She's the one," Eve said.

"Where has she been since his death?"

"New York, mostly. She's just starting to go out again. She asked to meet you. I couldn't fit you into dinner. So…" She shrugged, as if she needed to say nothing more to explain my presence there.

"If I'd known, I would have come earlier. She's stunning."

"Yes, isn't she?" Eve said, her tone flat and strangely non-committal.

"Why *does* she want to meet me?" I asked.

"You'll have to ask Mirella," she said, and left the bedroom.

I lingered to comb my hair, which had been whipped about by the wind on Riverside Drive. It gave me a few moments to adjust to this development. It was flattering, certainly, but also somewhat surprising. While I was at that point an available male, I wasn't, as far as I knew, an unusually desirable one; presentable enough, perhaps, but not the dashing type who received perfumed letters. As a published novelist, I was sometimes given attention by very young women with literary inclinations—naive English-major types, fresh from college. But I would hardly seem to justify the interest of a stylish Italian aristocrat.

Tobias Walling had been more appropriate for her: a distinguished Middle Eastern scholar, a millionaire, a name on the letterhead for almost any good liberal cause, and a civilized lover of all things antique. It would have been a good match—if the marriage had ever actually taken place.

I had heard the story—the bare facts, anyway, which were as much as anyone seemed to know. Walling was about to marry Mirella Ludovisi; the wedding was only weeks away. He went to stay with her at her family home, a palazzo in Ferrara. One morning he was found dead in his bed.

A heart attack, the obituaries said. For all those who knew him— and I, too, was slightly acquainted with him—the news was shocking and totally unexpected. Tobias Walling was only forty-eight years old, and seemingly in perfect health.

A rich American's sudden death in a palazzo. A dark-haired, pale-skinned countess who evoked a vanished world of cool marble and rustling silk. It sounded like pure Henry James.

And now that same bereaved beauty had expressed an interest in getting to know *me*. It was intriguing, and I was no less curious than old Henry himself would have been. With my hair in place, the knot of my necktie straightened, I went out to pay my respects.

Mirella Ludovisi was sitting in an armchair at one end of the couch. The corner of the couch nearest her was unoccupied and I settled into it.

"I'm Carl Hopkins," I said.

"I'm Mirella," she said.

She regarded me gravely. Her gaze was steady and somewhat unsettling, and it kept me from continuing in the usual glib, small-talk way. I said nothing further, simply sitting there, smiling at her, and waiting for her to break the silence.

"You're happy," she said.

"Happy?" In my own opinion, I was miserable. But perhaps she knew something I didn't.

"Yes, happy," Mirella repeated. "You seem happy. Life is good for you, is it not?"

This wasn't the time to beat my breast. So I replied, "Things could be worse, I guess."

Now, at least, she smiled, as if it pleased her to hear her estimate of my well-being confirmed. In a way her smile was sadder than her solemn look. It was a contained smile: the corners of her mouth barely moved, and her eyes didn't crinkle, didn't change at all, but remained wide-open, stark as the eyes of a prophetess.

"And is life a little better for *you* now?" I asked.

"It will be," Mirella said. "There will be felicity soon, I am sure of it."

She had answered promptly. But then she looked at me questioningly, as if she was uncertain as to what I had actually meant. "Do you know why I'm wearing black?"

It hadn't struck me that she was "wearing black" as such, since her dress didn't suggest mourning, but, rather, was a chic, Chanel-type black. The neckline curved gracefully to reveal the beginning curve of her bosom. "Yes, I know," I answered.

"This is my last night for black. I have some very pretty dresses, in all the nicest colors. It will be spring in a few days. It's time for me to wear them."

"You probably should have worn them long before this," I said. "You're too young and attractive to live in mourning."

Mirella was silent again, but her eyes didn't stray from my face. She seemed to be searching for hidden implications in my casual flattery. "Did you know Toby?" she asked finally.

"Only slightly," I replied. "But enough to find him very impressive."

"Yes," she said, "He was clever."

It seemed an odd way to put it. "Brilliant" perhaps or "scholarly." But "clever" was not an adjective one would normally have applied to the idealistic, romantic Tobias Walling.

But then, I reminded myself, English wasn't her native tongue, though it was easy to overlook this with her, since she spoke it flawlessly, with only a slight accent. It was her occasional peculiar choice of a word—*felicity*, for instance—that revealed that she wasn't totally at home in the language.

"He was one of the most erudite men I've ever met," I said.

She nodded. "I learned so much from him," she said.

So far she had said nothing to resolve the mystery of why she had supposedly wanted to meet me. I tried going at it more directly. "By the way," I asked, "have we seen each other before?"

"No," she said, "I don't think so."

"I wondered. You seemed to recognize me when I came in."

"Oh, I *know* you, yes," Mirella said softly, leaning closer to me. "I recognized you from your picture. On your book."

So *that* was it. She was a reader. I had been so caught up with my image of her as a Henry James princess, wandering through marble halls, that it hadn't occurred to me she might be a bored, urban woman who whiled away her evenings reading sexy commercial novels.

I knew she had to be referring to the sexy one, the most recent of my books, not the four more literary works that had preceded it. When people said "your book" it was the one they meant. It had reached a fairly wide readership, whereas my others had been well-kept secrets.

I adopted my wry, self-deprecatory stance. "I'm amazed you could recognize me from that photograph. It gave me all the warmth and charm of a zombie."

She didn't seem to know how to take this. "You didn't choose it?"

"My editor did. I think, in his heart of hearts, he hates me."

"But it captures something about you," Mirella said, "truly it does." The knowing gleam in her eye made me a little nervous. What on earth had she perceived in that ghastly photo? But then she added, with a touch of flirtatiousness, "Of course, now that I see you, I realize you're much better-looking."

"Thank you. I hope you liked the book," I said, an author outrageously fishing for a compliment.

"I liked it very much. After I read it, I knew I must meet you."

"Well, now we've met."

"Yes. And now that we've met," she said, rising, "I'm afraid I must go."

I was dismayed by the swiftness of it. Was I such a disappointment? I rose quickly. "Already?" I asked.

"It's late." She was taller than I had realized. Now that she was standing, and raised on high heels, her gaze was almost level with mine. "I would have gone long before this. But I was waiting for you to arrive. To see if you would be as I had imagined."

"Am I?"

"You are."

Once again, as with her comment on my author photograph, I was made to feel a little uneasy. How would she have imagined the author of my raunchy and somewhat cynical book?

"But you can't really know," I said. We've hardly had a chance to talk."

"Oh, we'll talk," Mirella said quietly, meaningfully. "But not now. Later. When we can be alone."

"May I call you?"

"*I'll* call."

"You promise?"

"You can be sure of it. You see," she added, "I want to discuss something with you."

I opened my mouth to ask "What?" but before I could get it out she was gone, vanished in a fluid movement that took her around the turning of the wall and out of sight.

2

I was starting to feel like a fraud.

After the usual disorganized youth, spent first as a high school teacher and then as a free-lance writer for magazines, I had put out my shingle as a novelist. I had assumed that, whatever its economic disadvantages, it was a lifetime vocation. There could be no forced early retirement, no office politics to drive me out into the cold. I would pass the years pleasantly, turning out a series of well-tooled narratives until I could no longer lift two fingers above my keyboard.

But the process had abruptly stopped. The landscape of my creative imagination had become a disaster area.

I kept it to myself. When people asked me what I was working on, I invariably replied brightly, "Oh, another novel, what else?" But it was a desperate sham. I had nothing about to come out. There was nothing in the pipeline, either.

I had thought the ideas would always come, that my powers of invention were limitless, that I couldn't possibly live long enough to write everything that, in the course of time, would spark into existence in my head. But I realized now that I had never been a great thunderclap-of-inspiration man. I had simply drawn upon the meager stock of my own experience.

I had written the coming-of-age-in-the-Pacific-Northwest novel, the frustrations-of-teaching-high-school novel, the unhappy-first-marriage novel, the young-artist-living-by-his-wits novel. And then I had written the big commercial book, basing my heroine on an opportunistic woman executive I had known in the magazine field; a ruthless-bitch-screws-her-way-to-the-top saga. That was the one that had done well; it had been selected by a book club and had had a largish paperback sale.

But that book had come out almost a year before. In the year and a half since I had completed it, I hadn't been able to dream up anything else. My problem—I had once thought it a virtue—was that I could only write effectively about things that, to some extent at least, I had absorbed first in life itself. This was all right if you were André Malraux or Ernest Hemingway, but it could put you in a hell of a fix if you were Carl Hopkins, former schoolteacher from Eugene, Oregon. I had already told my few stories, had gone through my short list of interesting people. There seemed to be nothing left. I was a dry well.

I wished now I were one of those facile fabricators who could spin out a yarn on virtually any subject. I wasn't, but it wasn't for lack of trying—and I went on trying. That morning, the morning after Eve Lukas's dinner party, I scarcely gave any thought to the beautiful woman I'd met the night before, with her air of mystery and suggestion of invitation. I was too disciplined for that kind of mooning. Instead, I went straight to my workroom, with a cup of strong black coffee in hand, and settled in to concentrate on the outline I was trying to hammer out—a CIA thriller in which the agent hero, with the help of Israeli intelligence, saved the President from an ingenious assassination attempt by Arab terrorists.

It didn't work. It seemed to work even less now than the last time I had gone over it—and I hadn't liked it then, either. It was forced, empty, lacking authority. How *could* it have any authority when I had no personal knowledge of the spook world? How could I compete with all those ex-CIA agents, many of them living comfortably on secret pensions, who were grinding out spy thrillers, the kind this one was intended to be, but sneaking in gimmicks, bits of color, that only *they* could know? I was put at a serious disadvantage. I hadn't gone to an Ivy League university. At my pinkish, small, liberal arts college in Portland no CIA recruiter had ever come by. It wasn't fair.

I threw the outline onto my growing discard pile, where it joined the other dud outlines—the roman à clef about the nymphomaniac movie star, the police manhunt for the sex killer. Feeling suddenly oppressed within the confines of my tiny workroom, I rose and went out to the living room.

I did it to clear my head. My living room had a spaciousness, an openness that could be therapeutic. It was a corner apartment, with unimpeded views in two directions, west to the Hudson and south to the World Trade Center. Sometimes when, after a long stint of work, I came up for air, it would revive me just to stand at a window. It gave me the sense of being a suddenly unfettered bird, perched high above Abingdon Square.

That didn't happen now, though. As I considered the Greenwich Village cityscape spread out around me, I felt as trapped by it as by the walls of my workroom. I wanted to be thousands of miles away, to be something very different. But at the age of forty-three what else could I be other than what I was? I had been too long out of teaching to get back into it, and the idea of it was unbearable, anyway. Otherwise, I was unemployable. There was no turning back; I was irrevocably committed to what I was doing, telling stories for a living—even though I no longer had any story to tell.

There was one hope of escape, one chance for a new life, a change of scenery. But that hope, once so fair, was starting to dim.

I had met with a young Hollywood producer—a "baby mogul," as they were called—who was interested in having me develop a screenplay from an idea of his. Tim Kellogg was his name and he purported to be an admirer of my recent novel. But as we sat over drinks at the Helmsley Palace, and I listened to him explain his shred of an idea—a rock star's disintegration and suicide—I began to have my doubts that he had read my book, or any other book, for that matter. He couldn't have been more than twenty-seven or twenty-eight, though he was already combing his hair forward to conceal a receding hairline, and he had a mind that snapped out empty ideas like the popping of bubble gum. At one point, he informed me that he was "nonverbal," at another point that he was "nonlinear," and by the end of the conversation I felt not only verbal and linear but also very old.

Nevertheless, I managed to sound cooperative and enthusiastic. I didn't want to blow this one. This was to be my ticket to a sunnier clime, where I would be ridiculously well-paid for doing nothing more that writing some itty-bitty lines of dialogue that took up only the middle third of a page.

At the time, I thought I had landed it. But I hadn't heard, and over the years I had learned that no news is not necessarily good news. Still, as I went out for my morning walk, I was careful to turn on my answering machine. I didn't want to miss a call from my agent.

I paused in the lobby to check the mail. Leafing through the envelopes, I saw that the bulk of it was uninteresting. Except for a small one that was, as the sender had meant it to be, upsetting on sight. It was from my ex-wife, Nadine.

I didn't hear from her too often; usually, it was her lawyer who wrote me. But when Nadine wanted to put on some extra pressure she would give it the personal touch and write to me directly. This, obviously, was one of those times. I ripped open the envelope to find out what the latest crisis was.

It was Jeffrey's teeth, as I should have known. We had been over that issue already, but Nadine wouldn't let up on it. In her letter, she stated her side of the case all over again, even more coldly than her lawyer might have. Not only was I supposed to provide for our son's support and education, she pointed out, but I had also agreed to pay for all of his medical and dental expenses. Jeffrey was having his teeth straightened and I had yet to send a check to cover any part of the swelling dental bill.

"I know how hard it is for you to think of anyone but yourself," her letter concluded acidly. "But, this once, please try to live up to your responsibilities. I can no longer accept your excuses that you don't have the money, since, as we all know, you have finally managed to write a successful book."

I resisted the impulse to crumple up the letter and fling it aside. Instead, I slipped it back into its envelope and returned it to the box along with the unopened mail. Then I went out and took a walk.

It was a very clear, brink-of-spring day, cold but with an exciting brightness. I walked to the Morton Street pier and back, a picturesque stroll in any weather. But I saw little and enjoyed none of it. I had been left too angry by Nadine's letter.

If Jeffrey had been sick, I would have scraped up every cent I could find to make sure he had the best of care. But straightening his teeth was a cosmetic thing, and unnecessary, I thought, since the kid's teeth had looked all right to me before. Seen with an objective eye, he was an ordinary-looking fourteen-year-old, and there was no compelling reason to give him the smile of a male model. Certainly not if it was going to cost a fortune in orthodontist's fees.

And did Nadine really think I had the money? After living with me all those years, she should have known how royalties work. The publisher might have made some money from my last novel, but I had seen little of it so far. The system was set up to delay payment. When my earnings were finally disbursed, the money would all go to repay the debts I was incurring. I would be broke again, with or without Jeffrey's teeth.

Nadine understood, all right. And she probably realized that, in her new existence as a real estate agent in Connecticut, she was more financially secure than I was. But it didn't matter; she was out to punish me. She had made that her life's work, to nurture her hatred of me, to get back at me.

I had been so unwise as to write that unhappy-first-marriage novel while I was still married. Nadine, it turned out, had as much difficulty separating fiction from reality as any average reader. Our marriage, which was already shaky, suddenly turned into a nightmare. I was forced to move out even before my novel reached the bookstores.

Not that the end hadn't been inevitable, anyway; we had grown too far apart. I would have offered as advice to any postadolescent, budding novelist that he should never marry his college sweetheart. A novelist creates himself anew, in much the same way as he creates his characters. A college-sweetheart-turned-wife remains essentially the same, just older and heavier.

Well, that was bitter, middle-aged wisdom, and it related to the past. The current problem could be neutralized—with money. Which was why Tim Kellogg and his tragic rock star movie had taken on such an importance to me.

When I returned to my apartment, the red light on the answering machine was on. I quickly played back the message. Maury, my agent, had called.

I dialed his number. The secretary put me through to him instantly and Maury, when he came onto the line, didn't waste time on pleasantries. "I heard from Tim Kellogg," he said.

"And?"

"Yes and no."

"What do you mean—yes and no?"

"He's interested in working with you. But he has some hesitations."

"Which are?"

"He's not sure you're contemporary enough. I mean, he doesn't know if you're tuned in with the coke generation."

"Is that like the Pepsi generation?"

"Don't get facetious, Carl. This is business."

"Okay," I asked, "what's the upshot?"

"The upshot is that he wants to know if you'd consider working with another writer on this."

"Who?"

"He has someone in mind. A young rock critic who's written a couple of screenplays."

"Produced?"

"No . . . but interesting stuff, according to Kellogg. He says he's a very with-it kid."

"Does he have his high school diploma yet?"

Maury was silent for a moment. Finally, he said, "If you're saying no, tell me."

"I'm saying no. You know I don't collaborate."

"That's your choice. Look, as far as *I'm* concerned, I think you should write another novel. The sooner the better. You agree?"

"I agree. Thanks, Maury." I hung up.

I was back on square one. I had to come up with a new novel; there were no other viable options for me.

But *what* novel?

3

The next morning Mirella Ludovisi phoned me.

"Is this Carl?"

"Yes."

"This is Mirella."

"Oh, hi, Mirella. How are you?"

"I'm fine, thank you." She paused. "Are you alone?" she asked, with uneasiness in her voice.

What did she expect? I wondered. That I might have an overnight visitor lingering?

"Yeah," I said, "I'm alone."

"I told you I would call," she said. She sounded more relaxed now, almost seductive. "Did you believe I would?"

"I thought you might."

"I've been thinking about you, Carl."

She didn't say this casually, but with a certain dramatic intensity. It stopped me for a moment. But then it occurred to me that this might be Italianate theatricality on her part, an exaggeration of a normal friendly interest.

"Well, I've been thinking about you, too, Mirella."

"We have much to talk about."

"Yes, I'm sure we do."

"Can you lunch with me tomorrow? At my house?"

"Yes, I'd love to."

"It will be the first day of spring. We can celebrate it together."

"Terrific."

She gave me the address and then, with a half-whispered *"Ciao,"* hung up.

There was no getting her out of my mind now, and for the rest of the day my thoughts kept returning to Mirella. And I found myself remembering her late fiancé, Tobias Walling.

My memories of him were fragmentary. While I had seen him around over the years, as one does in literary New York, at large gatherings—promotional events, fund-raisers for noble causes—I had actually talked with him only three times: first, briefly, at one of Eve Lukas's parties; the second time, more extensively, when we had dinner at a Village restaurant with our mutual friend, Alex Satin. Denny was with me on that occasion. It was during one of those periods when our romance was on.

Walling was a most engaging dinner companion. With his round, smooth face and his few strands of thin, silky hair, he suggested a constantly delighted baby, and he was quick with witty, informed opinions on almost every subject: the wine we were drinking, Greek folk customs—it was a Greek restaurant—the friends we had in common.

It was one of those rare evenings when Alex Satin didn't try to dominate the conversation. He didn't hold forth on his own projects, or fulminate against the commercial producers who stood in the way—or so he felt— of progress in the theater, who denied opportunities to experimental directors such as himself. He didn't bring up his own concerns at all. He deferred to Walling, as he deferred to few people, and allowed him to do most of the talking. It was a sign of the affection and respect he felt for the friend he had known since they were students together at Harvard.

Denny was obviously impressed with him, too; a little flirtatious, in fact, but this time I didn't let myself get jealous. The attentions of attractive women seemed Tobias Walling's natural due, just another blessing in a charmed life. On reaching manhood, he had come into five or six million dollars of a Yankee industrial fortune—an inequitable head start, perhaps, but, in his case, one didn't begrudge it him. With his good nature, his concern for the oppressed, his infectious love of life, and a powerful mind that had mastered five languages and as many cultures, it seemed an inheritance well applied.

Somehow he had managed to remain a bachelor through most of his adult years. There had been an early, brief marriage to an Iranian girl, when he had been at the beginning of the research for his book on sixteenth-century Persian culture. Since then, there had been numerous lovers, but no more wives.

Perhaps it was the fact that he was always traveling, absorbing the wonders of distant, exotic lands. Or that he had no real interest in family life. Or perhaps it was the romantic in him that wouldn't permit him to settle for any readily available mate but would lead him to search endlessly for the unattainable perfect woman.

Whatever the reason, it was a little surprising when, the third time I spoke with him, Tobias Walling announced to me that he was about to get married.

We had run into each other on a midtown street. I don't think he remembered my name, but he seemed to be bursting with his happy news and he told it to me at once. When I asked him who his future wife was, he answered, with fervor, "The most wonderful girl in the world!"

"Would I know her?"

"I doubt it." With a playful air of mystery, he said, "She's a fairy princess who lives in a faraway palace."

I thought he was simply waxing poetic, and I didn't pursue it. But the next week he left for that "faraway palace," the Ludovisi palazzo in Ferrara. It was his last journey.

So this wasn't just any lunch date with an attractive young woman. Even though Mirella was coming out of mourning, the atmosphere of tragedy remained. And, for some reason, from the midst of it, she was reaching out to *me*.

It gave this experience a savor, a sense of mystery. I felt a tingle of anticipation, and some uncertainty also, when, at the appointed time, I arrived at Mirella's address. It was as if I were about to step onto a stage to play a scene, but without knowing my role and having only the vaguest notion of the drama that was being enacted.

When I got out of the taxi, I paused to look up at the building. It was an actual private house, four stories high, on East Eighty-fourth Street, in the more remote part of Yorkville near the river, on a block that had been untouched by the developers. Mixed in with conventional Manhattan brownstones were a few old wooden houses that looked as if they might have been lifted intact from a New England town. Mirella's house was one of these. It was somber-looking, darkened by a century of weathering.

I went up the stairs and rang the doorbell. I was let in by a plump maid with a Spanish-Indian look to her. She didn't say anything when I stated my name and my reason for being there, and I suspected that she knew little or no English. She simply led me into the living room and disappeared.

I sat and took in the decor of the room. It wasn't quite what I had expected; not Northern Italian elegant, or even New York contemporary chic. Rather, it suggested the Middle East. A Persian rug, with a very elaborate design, was under my feet. The decorative objects on display included blue narrow-necked glass bottles, amber glass vases, large plates, standing on edge, lavishly decorated with floral patterns; all of them with the appearance of great age. A page from an illuminated manuscript was in a frame on the wall. The lettering, I guessed, was Persian. The painted borders showed a hunting scene; there were deer and dogs and turbaned men with curved blades. In a corner of the living room, a chess set, with enormous ivory pieces, rested on a teakwood table.

It dawned on me that this was Tobias Walling's living room. I vaguely remembered having heard that he owned a house in New York, and this, I realized now, was it. Mirella, evidently, was presently living in it. Was she just looking after the place? Or was she settled in more permanently?

Mirella came into the living room. I rose. She crossed to me swiftly and clutched my hand. "I am so glad you're here," she said.

It wasn't the conventional pleasantry. She said it as if she really meant it.

"Of course I'm here," I said. "Did you think I might not come?"

"I wasn't sure. I can never be sure in this city. Not now." She said nothing further to explain this cryptic statement, but asked, "What would you like to drink?"

After the usual back-and-forth chat about possible beverages, I settled on a glass of white wine. Mirella left the room to convey my request to the maid.

I heard them talking in the hall. It was an extended dialogue, longer than a drink order would seem to require. But since the conversation was in Spanish, I couldn't make it out. Mirella's Spanish, as best I could tell, was very good. She was obviously something of a linguist.

Mirella returned and sat beside me on the couch. "Lunch will be a little delayed," she said. "Profiria is slow today. She's upset. She's in trouble again."

"Trouble?"

"Pregnant."

"Oh."

"I'll pay for the operation. I always do." With a wry smile, she looked at me sidewise and said, "Her sex life seems to be livelier than mine."

The maid brought in two glasses of white wine on a tray. Mirella and I each took one. Mirella clinked her glass against mine. *"Salute,"* she said.

She kept her eyes on me as she sipped her wine. And I looked at her with equal interest. In the midday light of the living room, she seemed even more beautiful. The melancholy pallor was mostly gone; there was color in her complexion now, warm, youthful hues that went with the bright festiveness of her orange-and-yellow spring frock. She was wearing her long hair loose. The longest strands almost touched her bosom.

We were sitting near each other—our knees were only a few inches apart—and suddenly I wanted to be even closer to her. But I resisted the impulse. I was aroused by her, but I couldn't be sure that there was anything other than a somewhat inexplicable curiosity behind her gaze.

I played it safe and continued the conversation with a polite, conventional compliment. "This is a beautiful house," I said.

"Yes, isn't it?"

"It was Tobias's, wasn't it?"

"Yes. It's mine now."

"You own it?"

"Toby left everything to me."

I was a little surprised, but I said nothing. It seemed unusual, to say the least. A brief romance, a tragically aborted engagement. One wouldn't have thought that there would have been time enough or reason to arrange a legacy.

Mirella changed the subject. "Tell me about yourself."

"What do you want to know?"

"Eve has told me little. You were married."

"Married once, Divorced now. A not uncommon circumstance these days."

"And there's a woman that you've been . . . close to." She looked at me questioningly. "Denise? Is that her name?"

"Yeah, Denise. Or Denny—that's what everyone calls her."

"And this relationship is . . .?" She left the question unfinished.

"Ended," I said. "As of two months ago. I'm sure Eve told you."

"Yes. I did know that. I would not have invited you here otherwise."

"Why not?"

Mirella smiled sweetly. "I would not have wanted to trouble your girlfriend."

"Okay," I said, "you can have a clear conscience now."

After a moment, she asked, "Why did she break up with you?"

"Maybe I'm not such a terrific package."

"Oh, but that can't be true," she insisted softly. "You're an attractive man. And you have an interesting mind. I could see that in your book."

I was relieved that the conversation had shifted away from my personal business to my literary output. I tried to keep it there. "What did you find interesting in my novel?"

"The way you look at life." She thought for a moment. "That woman in your book—is she a real person?"

"No, she's fictional," I replied. "But I drew from real life. She's a composite of several people I've known." It was my usually cautious, legally foolproof answer.

"You have her do some wild things." Her smile, as she gazed at me, was cool and contained, as if she was appraising me. "Are you wild—or do you have a wild imagination?"

26

"The latter, I guess. You know," I added, "there's more to that book than just *those* parts."

"I know. I've read it twice."

"Twice?" This was gratifying to hear, indeed.

"I've had time to read," Mirella said, the melancholy coming into her expression now, "these last few months."

"Of course, I understand. I know this has been a difficult time for you."

Mirella nodded gravely.

I felt I should show some respect for the gravity of her bereavement, so I stayed with the subject. "Have you had family around to help you through this?"

"I have no family," she said.

"None at all?"

"My father is dead. My mother—" She stopped.

"She's dead, too?"

"She is in China."

"China?" I echoed, with surprise. "What is she doing in China?"

"She is staying with her brother." Mirella's face was expressionless and her voice was very even. "He's a diplomat."

"Oh, I see."

She was silent for a moment. Then she said, "I will tell you more, Carl, when I know you better. I cannot talk about it now. The story of my family is a very sad one."

"Most family stories are sad," I commented.

This was true enough, but mainly I said it to challenge her, to prompt her to say more. And, to some extent, she responded.

"*My* story is horrible," Mirella said. "If you knew it, you might not want to see me again."

"Why?"

She didn't answer, and her dark, tragic gaze told me I should ask nothing further. Whatever it was, clearly she felt it couldn't be brought up in ordinary conversation.

"Let's not talk about this any more," she said, her manner suddenly brisk. "I want to show you something."

She rose, crossed to a cloth-draped table, reached under it, and came up with a box. It was a ream box, the kind that contains manuscripts. She returned with it and sat beside me again.

"What's this?" I asked.

"Toby wrote it," she said.

She removed the cover of the box. There was no title page and I saw the first page of the manuscript. There was a fair amount of dialogue on the page. It seemed to be fictional dialogue.

"It's a novel?" I asked.

"Yes. It's not finished. Toby was still writing it."

"I didn't know he wrote fiction."

"He was attempting it," Mirella said. "He would talk to me about this book. It seemed to mean a great deal to him."

"Have you read it?"

"Yes." With a modest shrug, she added, "But I am no expert."

I was starting to get the point of this. "And you want *me* to read it?"

"If you wouldn't mind, Carl. It's my responsibility now, all of the writing Toby left. I want to do the right thing."

"And his writing belongs to you now?" I asked, to confirm what she had already suggested.

"Yes, it's all mine," Mirella said, with a note of possessiveness that seemed a little odd, since she was referring to a literary estate of presumably modest value. "I have been going through his papers. It's a big job, believe me," she said, making a weary face. "Most of it is scholarly work. Those manuscripts I will give to some university library. And there is his journal—" She paused and the small smile appeared that I was coming to think of as her secret smile; her lips stayed together and the corners of her mouth just barely turned up. "I don't know what to do with that. But then there is *this*," she said, patting the ream box.

"You want to know if it's publishable?"

"It would have to be completed, of course. By someone very professional. Like *you.*"

28

This was turning out to be a tremendous letdown. This beautiful countess wasn't offering me a romantic adventure, after all. She wanted to retain me for a hack writing job.

"Well, I'll look at it," I said.

"I would be so grateful, Carl," she said, taking my hand and squeezing it. "It's not for the sake of the money. I think it's what Toby would have wanted."

Her knee was touching mine now, she was looking almost hungrily into my eyes, and once again I was uncertain. What Tobias Walling might have wanted might not be what this was really about. I had a feeling that Mirella herself was after something more than just a heavy editing job from me.

The maid appeared in the archway and nodded.

"Now, let us have our lunch," Mirella said.

4

As a writer of fiction, Tobias Walling had been an amateur. I recognized that after reading only a few pages of the manuscript. But I read on, not simply to keep my promise to Mirella, but also because I was curious to find out what this unfinished novel might tell me about its author.

It was clearly autobiographical, a barely disguised rehashing of his childhood. But he had executed it as a beginner would, with no distancing from his material and with little artful selection. It was all there, the story of his adolescence; the prep school experiences, the summer vacations on the Cape, the close friendship with a classmate—a relationship he had presented, with surprising frankness, as quasi-homosexual.

The story, insofar as there was any continuous story at all, centered on the hero's divorced mother and her protracted affair with a handsome young man. The boy was in constant jealous agony over it. He saw the lover not only as a rival but as a calculating fortune hunter.

The main problem of the book, aside from the stiff, pedantic style, was his depiction of the mother. Walling obviously had adored his mother, had worshipped her uncritically. So the character that emerged was a saint, a victimized madonna. This was hardly acceptable as a credible interpretation of a lusty socialite, who had probably been no less self-indulgent and contradictory than others of her kind. But Walling evidently had been incapable of recognizing the falsity of his portrayal. It was as if he had remained frozen in the attitudes of a mother-loving fifteen-year-old boy.

The manuscript was riddled with apostrophes to the woman, to her beauty, her instinctive genius, her goodness, her enormous capacity for love. At one point, Walling stated it flatly—"The most wonderful woman in the world"—and I was reminded of his enthusiastic, and almost word-for-word identical, description of Mirella, the last time I saw him, just before he took his fatal journey to Ferrara.

When I finished, I put the manuscript back into its box and set it on the side table beside my armchair. Then I just sat for a few minutes and thought. I wondered again about Mirella's motivations in giving this unfinished work to me. She had told me she was an avid reader, so I assumed she knew an entertaining, effective novel when she saw one. Did she actually believe I could turn this into a publishable book?

It was remotely possible, of course. The story situation was workable and a total rewrite might make it into something. But there seemed to be no compelling reason to do so. Unless Mirella was determined to realize every last possible dollar from the Tobias Walling estate.

But this didn't make sense, either. The proceeds from a middling novel would be small potatoes to someone who had just inherited millions of dollars. It didn't seem to be worth the bother.

And then there was the other possibility, the one that had occurred to me when I was with her—that this manuscript might be, in fact, of no great importance to Mirella, and she had other reasons for getting to know me, reasons she had yet to reveal.

Well, whatever her reasons, I was willing to go along with this, for the time being, anyway. The woman intrigued me; I wanted to get to know *her*. So I opened my notebook and jotted down a few notes on possible revisions and a way of concluding the story.

It was late afternoon now, and I left my apartment to take a walk before the sunlight faded. But this time I didn't wander at random. I headed over to West Fourth Street, in the direction of Alex Satin's place. This business with Mirella had left some nagging questions in my mind, and I thought Alex might be the person who could answer them.

Alex, uncharacteristically, lived on a picturesque block that consisted entirely of small, very old brownstones that had the look of toys to them. As the declared enemy of all things cute, it would have seemed more appropriate for him to reside in some severe, Bauhaus-inspired, modernist structure. But he had lived on the parlor floor of a flaking little crackerbox of a house ever since I had known him. It was rent-controlled, after all.

When the weather was mild, I could usually tell, just by glancing up at his windows, whether or not he was home. If he was in his apartment, rather than teaching a class at NYU or directing one of his Off-Off-Broadway workshops, all the windows would be open. Alex was an asthmatic and he had a constant need for fresh air. But when he was out, the windows would be closed and locked. He also had an abiding fear of burglars.

When I stopped in front of his house, I saw that the windows were open.

"Alex?" I called up.

After a moment he appeared in a window. He had a rather distraught look on his face. "Oh, hello, Carl," he greeted me tensely.

"May I chat with you for a few minutes?" I asked.

"I have the maid here," he said.

"I won't get in her way."

"All right, come on up." He disappeared.

I went up the stairs to the front door of the house. Alex buzzed me in. He was waiting for me at the end of the hall, by the open doorway of his apartment. As I came up to him, I was about to extend my hand, then thought better of it. Alex, I could see, was in one of his fits.

A spasm of wrath suddenly went through him. "That bitch!" he cried out, in a strangled voice. "That unsavory bitch!"

He had briefly jerked his head around toward the open doorway, as if he was referring to someone in his apartment. "Who?" I asked, a bit confused. "The maid?"

"No, not her," Alex said. "Janice! The Great Whore Janice!"

He went back into his apartment and I followed him into the living room. The maid wasn't in there; she was working in the bathroom at the other end of the apartment, or so the sound of running water indicated. She evidently had already finished with the living room, since it looked about as neat as it ever could. The framed sketches of theatrical sets—Alex designed his own productions—seemed dust-free. The stacks of books on the floor had an uncharacteristic straightness to them.

Alex didn't offer me coffee or a drink, or even, for the next few moments, any acknowledgment of my presence there. He simply paced around the room, plucking agitatedly at his small dark curls of hair. He had the spare frame of someone whose fat is eaten away by his own bilious passions and now as this latest rage worked within him, he seemed gaunter than ever.

I patiently waited for him to come out with it, to inform me what offense Janice, his current love, had committed against common decency in general and Alex Satin's psyche in particular.

"She's been telling me," Alex said abruptly. "She's been telling me the disgusting things she's been doing with that Swede of hers!"

I knew that Janice, though sleeping with Alex, was carrying on a simultaneous affair with a Swedish businessman. But I hadn't been aware that she was so open about it. "Janice has been telling you?"

"No, not Janice," Alex replied impatiently. "The maid."

"*This* maid?" I asked, lowering my voice. The water had stopped running in the bathroom, and I couldn't be sure she wasn't listening.

"Yes, this one. Thelma."

"Why would she know about Janice?"

"Because she's *her* maid, too." Alex's face twisted in an almost ecstatic agony. "Thelma's been filling me in on all the revolting details."

"How could she know them? Do they let her watch?"

"Damned near! There's nothing delicate about them, those two. They don't stop what they're doing when Thelma arrives to clean the apartment. Oh, no, they just keep rutting away. Then they come out half-naked, eat some yogurt, and go back into the bedroom and rut some more." Alex's voice dropped to a sickened near-whisper. "She can hear them when they come. Janice screams. The Swede laughs."

I didn't quite know what to say. Alex wasn't your typical pining lover. He was a middle-aged sensualist with equal measures of sadism and masochism in him—and the latter seemed to be in the ascendancy at this point. If his various girlfriends had ended up in other men's beds, it was perhaps understandable. They hadn't taken up with him, in the first place, in the spirit of true love. Usually, they were young women who, like Janice, had aspirations as actresses. Janice, a beautiful socialite, was classier than most of the others, but basically her motivation had to be the same; she hoped that Alex would provide a showy role for her that would lead to her being discovered. Certainly, she wasn't drawn to him because of his stability and tenderness.

Alex, however, insisted on treating each tacky affair as a grand, dark passion, and his friends had no choice but to humor him. So, striking the proper note of sympathy, I said, "You shouldn't torture yourself like this, Alex."

"What else can I do?" he asked.

"Well, you could get another maid."

Alex stared at me. "I wouldn't dream of giving her up! I *want* to know. I can't afford it—but I'm having her in three times a week."

"Just so you won't miss anything?"

"The Swede is going hot and heavy," he said grimly.

The maid appeared, wearing her coat. She was a thin, elderly black woman.

"Are you through?" Alex asked her.

"Yes, Mr. Satin."

"When can you come again?"

"Day after tomorrow, if you want me."

"Yes, yes, please come," Alex said eagerly. He took out his wallet, went to her, and thrust some bills into her hand.

"Thank you," the maid said, and crossed to the door. Before going out, she looked back and gave him a slightly wicked smile. "Have a nice day, Mr. Satin."

When the maid was gone, I decided it was time to bring up my own concerns. "Alex, I want to ask you about something."

"What?"

"May I sit?" He hadn't invited me to as yet.

"Of course."

I sat on the little sofa, which was worn though of good quality—a description that fitted almost everything in the apartment—and Alex sat in a chair opposite me. His mood had passed and he was a politely attentive host now.

"I had lunch with Mirella Ludovisi the other day," I began.

"You did?" His face darkened. "Why did you do that?"

"Because she invited me." I didn't know what to make of his negative reaction, so I asked, "Is there any reason I shouldn't?"

"You show a peculiar taste in the company you keep."

I was growing more puzzled. Since he had been Walling's friend, I had assumed that he was Mirella's too. "You don't see her?"

"I don't see her. I haven't talked with her since Tobias died."

"Not even at his memorial service?"

"I didn't speak to the creature. None of us did."

I looked at him uncomprehendingly. "What has she done wrong?"

He didn't answer the question. Instead, his expression impassive, he said, "You wanted to ask me something. What is it?"

"Oh—well, it's about the papers Tobias left." Alex's strange attitude had made me wary. So, rather than referring specifically to the novel, I couched it in vague terms. "Mirella has asked me to do some editing on them."

"I see," Alex said, nodding thoughtfully. "I imagine Tobias had some interesting work going. Have you had a look at any of it yet?"

"She gave me some of his writing to take home with me."

"Scholarly work?"

"No, it's of a personal nature. Quite interesting. But what I'm not sure about," I went on, "is the ownership of these papers. I don't want to do anything with them if I haven't been properly authorized. Mirella says Tobias left her everything—but that's hard to believe."

A thin, bitter smile came onto Alex's face. "Is it?"

"I mean, she knew him so short a time. How long was it? A year?"

"More like six months," he replied. "But she worked fast."

"Worked fast?" I echoed uncertainly.

"First, she got the poor man completely gaga over her. She's a good-looking piece. And she has a title. Tobias was a secret snob, you know. He was a sucker for a title."

"It had to be more than just that."

"Of course, there were other factors. I have to admit, Mirella is not without a certain deadly charm. And she was clever. She found the magic words to say to him."

"What were they?"

"She told him she wanted to have his baby."

"Not a very fresh notion."

"I shouldn't think so. But then I suppose Tobias's other women hadn't been too keen on maternity. Or it could be that Mirella caught him at the right time of life—when he was worrying about death—and, you know, starting to want whatever immortality he could find in passing on his genes."

"So he asked her to marry him?"

"And she accepted. But on one condition. He had to make out a new will at once. Which he did. In his old will, Tobias left most of his money to his mother, a couple of bequests to cousins he was fond of, the rest to good causes. In the new will, his mother, everyone, and everything else was cut out. The entire estate was left to Mirella."

"Didn't anyone try to talk him out of it?"

"No one knew. If his mother had heard about it, she would have raised hell. She'd hated Mirella from the beginning. But it was kept secret. And so," Alex went on, "the poor lovestruck fool made out his new will—and immediately flew off with Mirella to her palazzo. Two weeks later, he was dead."

Suddenly, I understood not only his hostility toward Mirella but her mistrustful seclusion as well. "My God, Alex, are you implying she murdered him?"

He shrugged. "Who can say? All I know is that Tobias, as far as anyone could tell, was in perfect health. And he had no history of heart trouble at all."

"But wouldn't the police have checked it out?"

"Yes," Alex said, with a short laugh, "the Italian police are always on top of things, aren't they? Anyway, Mirella is a Ludovisi—one of the hotshot aristocrats in Ferrara. Even in this day and age, I don't imagine the peasant cops question a countess too closely."

It was too shocking even to consider. Nevertheless, I stayed with the idea for a moment. "How would she have done it?"

"How did Lucrezia Borgia do it? Poison, I suppose. Things probably haven't changed too much in those Renaissance palazzos. They may still do business the old way."

I was appalled. Then, suddenly, I recognized the preposterousness of it. Alex was paranoid enough to be susceptible to conspiracy theories. But I felt I had a better grasp of reality.

"This isn't fair," I said. "People *do* get heart attacks without warning."

"No," Alex admitted, "maybe it isn't fair."

"The fact that there was a new will shouldn't have anything to do with it. It was just unfortunate timing."

"Unfortunate for Tobias, anyway," he said. "Not so bad for Mirella."

5

For the rest of that day, I couldn't stop thinking about it. Just imagining the sinister sequence of events that might have led up to Tobias Walling's death filled me with horror.

It was a chilling, fascinating possibility. More important, it was a story.

I realized now that it was what I had had at the back of my mind all along, from the time I had first met Mirella—the thought that there might be a story in her. I had sensed it about her even as she sat quietly in Eve's living room: Mirella was a woman of secrets. Dark secrets, perhaps. Beautiful and charming though she was, there was something vaguely frightening about her. You felt that she might be from some other world where the natural laws worked very differently, and that what was normal and acceptable to her could be deadly to you and your kind.

Which is not to say that I went along with Alex in his supposition. I thought it unjustified, highly unlikely. What his story had revealed to me was that Mirella was an opportunist. And that she had a greedy streak in her that belied her refined, ethereal persona. But nothing he had told me, and nothing that I already knew about her, gave me reason to believe that she was capable of murder.

I had learned a little more about her as we had our lunch. She had been in this country for twelve years, having originally come here for her college education—she was a bit older than I had thought; nearing thirty, if she wasn't already there. After graduating from Sarah Lawrence, she had remained in New York. She didn't seem to have any particular career goals, and, in the years since college, she hadn't had much in the way of regular employment; a period at the UN in some unspecified capacity, a shorter period working with an art dealer, and that was about it. She had done some translating for scholarly periodicals and Italian magazines. But for the most part, I gathered, she had lived a life of cultivated leisure, as the women in her family had for many generations.

An unremarkable history; it certainly didn't offer the profile of a murderess. But it didn't matter that I couldn't buy it as truth, that I didn't really believe that Mirella had done away with poor Tobias. The important thing was that it *could* have happened. As a writer of fiction, that was all I ever needed, the potential of an action. I left halting, formless actuality to the journalists.

The novel—the beginning lineaments of it, anyway—was starting to take shape in my mind, and I was getting excited. I was eager to learn more, to fuel my imagination with whatever solid substance real life had to offer.

And so, the next morning, I phoned Mirella and told her I was ready to discuss Tobias's manuscript. She seemed pleased and invited me over to her house for drinks at six.

That afternoon, I walked down to Soho to take in the galleries. I had become something of a culture junkie in the past year. Seeking distraction from the nagging ache of writer's block, I had gone to theatrical events and dance concerts, and I had attended most of the new art shows. An excursion through the galleries near where I lived was something I did at least once a week. It had become part of my routine.

But this time I cut it short. I only went to the Castelli gallery, and I didn't stay long. With a new book working in my head, I found I had lost interest in minimalist fields of color.

On the way back, I followed a route that took me across Washington Square. I did it more for the sake of variety, so I wouldn't retrace my steps, than for any affection I felt for that once charming but now blighted little park. As I approached it, I saw the usual present-day scene, an uneasy mix of the old Village and the new. There were the respectable citizens who had always been there, mothers with their infants, NYU students killing time, old people from the neighborhood sunning themselves; but there were also derelicts drinking from wine bottles in paper bags, stoned druggies sitting dazedly at the edge of the fountain, and a menacing-looking gang of ghetto teenagers loitering in a corner of the park, coolly eyeing each passerby.

As I started onto the main path, I encountered Sasha Rombeck. Or almost encountered her, I should say, since, as soon as she saw me, she took evasive action to avoid a meeting with me.

It was quite puzzling. I saw Sasha coming almost directly on a line with me, her long, straight hair stirring in the breeze, her expression self-absorbed. Then, as she recognized me, a stricken look came onto her face. She suddenly veered off in a tangent, quickening her pace.

What was the problem? I wondered. I knew of no reason why Sasha should have had either a positive or a negative reaction to me. I wasn't that close a friend and I certainly wasn't an enemy. And yet she had skittered away from me as she would have from a satanic presence.

The best thing seemed to be to ignore it, so I walked on without looking back. But I continued to think about it, trying to figure it out.

Sasha Rombeck was an attractive, efficient woman who worked for the Landmarks Preservation Commission. Trained as an architect, and probably quite shy by nature, she had developed, in the course of doing her job—which involved constant tricky maneuvering with the developers who were bent on tearing down New York's precious old buildings—a politician's affable manner. This smiling, reasonable woman was the only Sasha *I* knew, not the distraught creature who had just fled from me.

I had always hit it off with her before. She was statuesque and voluptuous, with, despite her business suits, a suggestion of underlying sensuality; but I had never touched her, so *that* couldn't have been the reason. I continued to be at a loss for the cause of her strange behavior.

There *was* a connection with my current preoccupation, I now remembered. Sasha had been the next-to-last woman in Tobias

Walling's life. She'd had a lengthy affair with him, until Mirella displaced her. But this seemed merely coincidental; I didn't know what it could have to do with me.

Still, I didn't understand what else it could be. It had to be, in some way, the answer. As I became more sure of it, I looked back over my shoulder to see if Sasha was anywhere in sight.

She was, in fact, very near. She had followed me back across the square and was walking quickly, as she hurried to catch up with me. I stopped by the Washington Arch and turned to her.

She didn't just come up to me. Rather, she confronted me, with desperation in her eyes. "Don't tell anyone!" she said intensely.

I was taken aback. "Don't tell anyone what?"

"If you tell anyone what you've read I'll hate you for the rest of my life!"

"What I've read?" I echoed puzzledly.

"Don't pretend you don't know! You can get your kicks, if you want—I can't stop you. But just keep it to yourself."

"I've no idea what you're talking about."

My bafflement must have seemed genuine enough to her, because she paused uncertainly.

"Toby's journal," she said.

"Sasha," I said reasonably, "I haven't *seen* Toby's journal. What makes you think I have?"

Her anger faded, but she wasn't ready to give up the idea yet. "Alex said so."

"Alex Satin?"

"He phoned me this morning. He said Mirella gave you Toby's journal—to do some kind of editing on it."

This made a little more sense to me. I wasn't surprised that Alex had phoned her; he was something of a gossip and he could be a troublemaker. I remembered telling him that the material Mirella had given me was "of a personal nature." But I didn't see why he had jumped to such an erroneous conclusion about it.

"She gave me a manuscript," I said. "But it wasn't his journal. It was a novel Tobias was working on."

"Oh." A different kind of unhappiness came onto her face, the discomfort of someone who feels she may have just made a fool of herself. "And that's *all* you've seen?"

"That's all. I can't imagine why Alex thinks I would have seen his journal, too."

"Because he knows," Sasha said, growing agitated again. "He knows she's been tormenting me."

"Tormenting you? How?"

"She calls me up and reads to me from Toby's journal—the parts where he wrote what we did together." Her face had reddened. Her hand went to her cheek and she looked away. "He shouldn't have written about those things!"

All I could do was wait, allow a few seconds for the pain of her awakened humiliation to subside.

At length, she looked up at me. "You didn't know, did you? You didn't know."

"No, I didn't."

"Oh, damn it!" she said, under her breath. She ducked her head and rushed away.

I watched her as she fled across Washington Square, a tall, competent woman who had lost her control, half running now like an unsteady child.

6

I didn't bring it up right away. I waited until we had finished our discussion of Walling's manuscript.

This actually didn't take too long. I told Mirella my thoughts on the book—muting my criticisms considerably—and she listened thoughtfully, saying little.

She made her only real comment when I stated my opinion about the character of the mother. She nodded vigorously in agreement with my point that the woman had to be presented as less of a plaster saint.

"Yes!" Mirella said. "Yes! Mothers are never so wonderful, are they? And *this* one—Toby didn't see it—but this one could eat you up alive!"

It seemed a strangely carnivorous image for the genteel lady in the book. But then I remembered Alex's saying that Mrs. Walling detested Mirella. The hostility obviously was mutual.

When I concluded my little discourse, I said, "Well, that's my analysis. I don't know if it's any help to you or not."

"Oh, yes," she insisted, "it's *very* helpful."

It was time to break the bad news to her gently. "You said you were hoping to find someone to complete this novel for you. If you want my honest opinion, I don't think it's worth the trouble."

A bit hesitantly, she asked, "Then *you* wouldn't consider it?"

"No, I'm afraid I don't have the time."

"Oh, very well," she murmured, "I understand."

She seemed disappointed, but not *too* much so, I noticed. It was as if my answer was what she had expected.

We were silent for a moment. Mirella was on the couch, not lounging on it but sitting straight and alert. She was wearing a clinging white dress with a slit in it that revealed most of a perfect leg. There was no trace now of the grieving maiden in black; her appearance was frankly sexually provocative.

I understood the meaning of her attentive look. She had already carried out her opening gambit. It was my turn to make a move.

"I hope I can see you again," I said.

"I would like that, Carl." She paused. "I need a friend."

"Well, I'd like to be your friend."

The fake kindliness of my statement aroused a twinge of guilt in me. I was a predator, hungry for this woman's secrets. If I wanted to avoid being a hypocrite, I would have to keep this on a strict boy-girl basis.

"May I take you out some night?" I asked.

"Yes."

"We can have dinner somewhere. Do you like to dance?"

"If *you* like to dance, I will dance."

"I'm a terrible dancer," I said. "I was just checking."

"Then we'll simply keep each other company," she said, with a smile.

We had a nice, warm mood going, and I felt it might be safe to bring it up now, the curious, disturbing thing I had learned on Washington Square that afternoon.

"Well, terrific," I said. "Then this isn't the end of it." Ease into it casually, I told myself. Make a joke out of it. With a little laugh, I went on, "I guess it's just as well I won't be working on Tobias's papers. People seem to misunderstand."

"What do you mean?"

"Oh, I ran into someone we both know today. Sasha Rombeck."

Mirella's face settled into an impassive mask. "Oh? And you talked about me?"

"Not really. But she'd heard I was going over some of Tobias's writing for you."

Her mouth tightened slightly. "How did she hear that?"

"Well, I mentioned it to Alex Satin—without telling him what it was. And somehow he got the idea that it was Tobias's journal.

Anyway, Sasha was pretty upset about it." I smiled at her. "It seems you're being naughty."

"In what way?"

"She says you've been calling her up and reading to her from his journal. Things about her. Personal things." Teasingly, I asked, "Are you really that wicked, Mirella?"

"Yes, I'm wicked," she said.

She had answered lightly, but her smile chilled me suddenly. There was no humor in her eyes, no playful mischief. Behind her fixed gaze, I recognized no companionable feeling at all; whatever was there was dark and unknowable. I sensed for a moment that I was being unwise, that, rather than trifling with this woman, I would be well advised to leave her house at once.

"I'm wicked," Mirella said, "but never without a cause."

"Sasha has given you cause?"

"Yes, she has given me cause. She has been talking against me."

"What has she been saying?"

"If you've spoken with Alex, you can guess what it is."

There was no reason for me to pretend ignorance. "The circumstances of Tobias's death?"

She nodded. Her face was pale with contained anger now. "You can't imagine what losing him meant to me," she said. "The pain has been unbearable. But the people like Sasha and Alex give no thought to my suffering. No, instead they accuse me of terrible things!"

I shrugged, as if it were of no great importance. "They're being silly, I think."

"Silly!" She repeated the word bitterly. "There must be some other way to say it. What is it when people try to destroy you with lies? They have killed Toby and now they want to kill me, too!"

"Mirella," I said gently, "you can't say they killed Toby."

"Oh yes, they *did!*" she insisted. "With the bad they wished on us. None of them wanted Toby to marry me—not Alex, not Sasha, and not that old hag, his mother. Their evil thoughts followed him; they stopped his heart!"

45

Mirella had said this with passionate conviction, and I realized that, for all her transatlantic sophistication, her veneer of aristocracy, she had something of the peasant in her—a primitive superstitiousness, a lingering belief in the evil eye that can blight anyone's good fortune, even snuff out a life.

"I won't argue with you," I said. "But maybe you should just forget about them."

"I am not a meek person, Carl," she said, with a sudden, icy calm. "I am not a gentle lamb. If someone is my enemy, I fight back. I punish."

"Is that what you're doing with Sasha?" I asked. "Punishing her?"

"Yes," she replied simply.

"By reading to her from an old lover's journal? I don't get it. Why should that be so terrible?"

She looked at me silently for a moment and the cool, small smile returned to her lips. "Let me show you something," she said, rising.

I rose, wondering what it was she wanted me to see. Mirella, without explaining further, started out of the living room, gesturing to me to follow.

We went up the stairway. The floor above, the third floor of the house, had a half-abandoned look to it. There were fresh flowers in a vase on a small table in the hallway, but that was almost the only sign of habitation. Up and down the hallway, doors were closed that must usually have been kept open. The single open doorway was at the rear, and I could see that it led into a master bedroom. It seemed to be the only room on that floor that was in use.

Mirella started down the hallway toward the bedroom. Before I followed, I paused to glance up the stairs at the floor above. But there was nothing I could see. For some reason, there was no illumination at all in the top-floor hallway. Only darkness, an even greater darkness than was justified by the time of evening. It was as if every curtain on that floor was drawn, obliterating any possibility of light.

I was struck not so much by the waste of space as by the sadness of it. Tobias Walling, I was sure, had found ways to make his whole house live. But Mirella seemed to be restricting herself to small, safe

46

areas in it, huddling in corners, leaving the greater part of the structure to dust and desolation.

We went into the bedroom, a conventional enough lady's boudoir. There was a raised four-poster bed, an antique piece that probably had belonged to Walling. But the rest of the furnishings in the room—the little chairs, the dressing table, the fluffy rugs, the silk hangings—were contemporary and feminine. I imagined that most of what was in that room had been brought by Mirella from wherever she had lived before, or purchased by her since.

Crossing to the closet, she took down a stack of black composition books from the shelf within and carried them over to the bed.

"Tobias's journal?" I asked.

"Yes," Mirella replied. She quickly checked through the composition books—some seven or eight—found the one she was looking for, and held it up. "Sasha's book. She is the star in this one."

"You're not going to read it to me, are you?" I asked.

"I have to," she said, missing the point—deliberately, I assumed—of my uneasy question. "Toby's handwriting is difficult. Only I can make it out." She flipped through the pages of the composition book, as if searching for a particular passage. "This Sasha—she is a great lady, no? She has meetings with the Mayor?"

"It's part of her job, yes."

"And she is from some very good family? In Maryland? Is that right?"

"Maryland sounds right."

She came to a stop at a page. "Sit, Carl," she said. "Listen."

I sat in a chair by the bed. Mirella crossed her legs under her and began reading aloud.

"'I lie back, exhausted. I'm hoping we are through. But soon Sasha is at me again, sucking me.'" Mirella's voice was uninflected, almost a monotone, but she was reading very precisely. Her accent had almost vanished and somehow, perhaps unconsciously on her part, she was suggesting Walling's cultivated New England speech. "'I try to push her away, but she doesn't let me. "Please, Daddy," she says, "please."' And I realize that the transformation has happened and I am now that other man to her. She lies back, pulling me onto her. Aroused, I enter her. Sasha is shaking, crying and moaning. she has become a frightened, ecstatic little girl and once again her father is raping her.'"

"I don't want to hear any more," I said.

Mirella looked up from the composition book, took in my discomfiture, and smiled. Then she read on.

"'It's wilder than it's ever been, we're in a frenzy. "Hurt me, Daddy!" she cries out. "I'm your little whore. Hurt me!"'"

"Stop!" I said. I rose quickly, snatched the composition book from her hands, and threw it aside on the bed.

I had done it impulsively, without thinking, and I was startled by my own action. But it had just been too obscene to bear for another moment, this flaunting of another person's painful secrets.

Also, as I dimly recognized, I may have reacted to what was happening in myself as I heard this sick, sad passage. In some shameful way, it had turned me on. Something dark and sensual was stirring in me.

And Mirella seemed to know it. She remained perfectly still, in the frozen moment after my abrupt action, as I hovered over her. Her face was quite close to mine. The smile was still on her lips and her gaze was burning into me.

I drew her to me and kissed her. It wasn't gentle; it had the violence of a spasm, the savagery of suddenly released desire. I put my hand to her breast and, though I had enough control of myself to caress it gently, what I wanted to do was dig my fingers into the flesh and make her scream with pain.

She leaned back, reached into her dress, lifted out her bare breast, and offered it to me. I took it in my hands and kissed it hungrily, sucked the erect red nipple.

Mirella allowed me to cling to her for a few seconds. Then she pushed me away. She had surprising strength.

"No," she said. "Not now. Not yet."

7

We started seeing each other regularly. In the next week, I took Mirella out three times; first to dinner, then to the theater, and to a party.

No affair had started as yet. In fact, after each date, Mirella kissed me good night at her door without inviting me in. Her properness was a little baffling to me; it was as if that moment of dropped inhibitions, of suddenly released desire, had never happened. But it had, and I was haunted by the memory of her offered breast, abidingly excited by it—and left wondering at the wantonness of the gesture. For an instant, she had seemed a practiced courtesan, not a sheltered aristocrat.

It had been a tantalizingly sensual beginning for our relationship, but, for the time being, we were on our good behavior. I didn't push things. I knew that, sooner or later, we would get back to the point— and go beyond it.

Our conversation, too, was somewhat circumscribed. Mirella spoke freely about her more distant past, about her privileged upbringing as the beloved only child of Count and Countess Ludovisi. The feudal tradition, I gathered, was still alive in her small part of the province of Emilia. The men in her family had always been soldiers and diplomats, and the income came in, as it had for centuries, from the rents paid by the tenant farmers who worked the Ludovisi ancestral lands. The Count himself had been a military man in his youth, an air force colonel, but he had withdrawn into the scholarly life. He had labored for years over his magnum opus, a history of the city of Ferrara—a book, I gathered, that had remained unfinished at the time of his death.

It was an idyllic way of life that Mirella portrayed. She described, quite colorfully, the customs that had survived: the ritual at harvest time, for instance, when the peasants would come with baskets filled with the best they had grown to give to the Count and Countess. It sounded like a charmed existence—if you lived in the palazzo, anyway—but one that was increasingly threatened by a sinister mass of people whose group name Mirella could hardly utter without making a face. The Communists.

When it came to her adult years, though, her time in this country, she had little to say. It wasn't that she avoided talking about this period—she did make references to this or that person who was a friend or acquaintance from her recent life—but she didn't seem to want to dwell on it. Her six months with Tobias Walling, she insisted, had been a blissful time for her. But this romantic interlude seemed to have been an exception, an interruption in the protracted malaise of her young womanhood. Living in New York, she implied, had not been a very happy experience for her.

Which made it all the more a mystery why she was here at all. If life in Italy had been so wonderful, why had she completely abandoned her own country to live in the urban blight of Manhattan? She had no career reason for it. And no other logical reason presented itself to my mind.

The answer to this, whatever it was, was Mirella's secret, and not her only secret, by any means. Rather than discovering, as I had half expected I would, that there was nothing very remarkable behind her enigmatic facade, I was getting a sense of secrets beyond my first reckoning, interlocking secrets, secrets underlying secrets.

Even so mundane a matter as what she did with her time when I wasn't seeing her was becoming something of a mystery. Obsessed as I was with her, I wanted to see her every evening. But sometimes she would put me off without giving any clear reason. She hinted that she had other obligations, but never specified what they might be.

That Sunday, for instance, at the end of my first week of going with her, I had a brunch invitation. Mirella told me that she was busy and couldn't accompany me. When I asked her what business she had on an early Sunday afternoon, she evaded the question, gave me no answer at all.

So I went to the brunch alone, with reluctance, now that I was deprived of Mirella's companionship—though, as a matter of fact, I brought a certain lack of enthusiasm to all brunches. They weren't my favorite occasions. I didn't like drinking at midday, nor was I partial to the combination of lox and scrambled eggs at any time.

This brunch was being given by my publisher's publicity woman. Acquainted with her only in a business capacity, I assumed I had been invited to serve as an ornament, one of her deliverable house authors. I didn't imagine I would encounter many people I knew there. When I arrived at the hostess's tiny West End Avenue apartment, it proved to be as I had expected. The group consisted of a few publishing types I knew only slightly and a larger number of people who were total strangers to me. But there was one exception. Eve Lukas, who had an uncanny knack for turning up unexpectedly at any gathering, was there too.

Eve was in the midst of a deep conversation with a handsome older gentleman who had an affluent look to him, so I didn't disturb her. I chatted, instead, with a lady novelist who was the other house author present. She wrote mildly racy romantic fantasies for mid-American, middle-aged women—the semiliterate portion of that public, if I was to judge from the one book of hers I had sampled. I found I had little to say to her. Her conversation was of a piece with her prose.

Eventually, the lady novelist asked the inevitable question. "What are you working on now?"

"I've got something pretty exciting going, I think," I replied.

The lady novelist's face tautened. Evidently, she wasn't one of *my* well-wishers, either. "Can you tell me what it is?"

"No, I'm afraid I can't. It's secret."

I finished my own Virgin Mary and then prepared to leave. I crossed to Eve Lukas, who had just completed her conversation with the handsome older gentleman and was turning away to move elsewhere. "I'm going now, Eve," I said. "Sorry we didn't get a chance to talk."

Eve gazed at me steadily for a moment. "Walk me home, Carl," she said. "We *should* talk."

There was no mistaking her meaning: she had something to say to me. I had no idea what it could be, but went along with her request. We said goodbye to the hostess and departed.

Eve's apartment building was only two blocks away on Riverside Drive. As we walked, she chatted lightly about a few of the people at the brunch. I didn't pressure her to get on to whatever more serious business was concerning her. She would bring it up, I knew, in her own good time.

Eve Lukas was one of those connective individuals without whom New York social life, in its free flow and variety, could not exist. She was the common link for any number of disparate people who otherwise would not have had any reason to know each other.

She herself, in her fifty years, had passed through several worlds without becoming permanently fixed in any one spot. First she had been an actress; then the home-keeping wife of a wealthy doctor; now she was a photographer. The magazines and advertising agencies gave her some work, though probably not enough to support her. This didn't seem to be a problem. Her divorce settlement, evidently, had left her well off.

Basically, Eve's lifework was the cultivation of people, though not friendships as such; she set limits that few crossed—the exploration of urban, sophisticated humanity in all its quirkiness. I don't believe that she felt any great, warm-hearted love for her fellow beings. What she did have was a keen curiosity, coupled with a tolerance so all-encompassing it could be called amoral.

I had known Eve for a number of years. I no longer remembered how I had first met her. It didn't matter. Sooner or later, Eve would have turned up in my life, as she had turned up in the lives of most of the people I knew.

When we got to her apartment, Eve took care of the beverage— glasses of Perrier for both of us—and then we settled down in her living room to talk.

"Have you seen Denny?" she asked.

"No, I haven't." Was that what this was all about? I wondered. Did she want to try to mend things between my ex-girlfriend and me? Was she hoping to be the savior of a romantic lost cause? "Have you?"

"I ran into her in Bloomingdale's yesterday," Eve said.

"How is she?"

"She *looked* wonderful. But she seemed a little frantic. They're keeping her busier than ever in her job."

"I'm sure." There was no way Denny could *not* be busy in her job. She was the talent coordinator for a television talk show. She did the pre-interviewing, and there was a nonstop flow of guests and prospective guests into her office—celebrities, demi-celebrities, or just nuts looking for exposure.

"She asked about you," Eve said.

"And you told her I was fine?"

"She wasn't inquiring about your well-being," she said dryly. "Someone saw you at the theater the other night with Mirella. The person called Denny to tell her about it."

"That's some terrific friend," I commented, "whoever that person is."

Eve gave me a look that would have been a sigh, if she had been given to sighs. "I wish Denny and you could get together."

I shrugged. "If it isn't to be, it isn't to be."

"The two of you are so right for each other."

"I think Denny would disagree. I might, too."

"Well, perhaps I'm not the one to judge. But I'm sure Denny is more right for you than Mirella." Her expression became quite serious. With quiet emphasis, she said, "I don't think you know how wrong for you Mirella is."

So this was what Eve had wanted to talk to me about. I didn't know what she assumed was going on between Mirella and me, but I thought it best to avoid the issue, to dismiss it lightly. "Why are you worrying about her?" I asked. "I barely know the lady."

"You've been seeing her regularly, haven't you?" Eve asked. She's more than just a casual acquaintance by now?"

"Yes, you could say that," I admitted.

"But you're not in deep yet?"

"No, I'm not in deep."

"Good," she said. "Don't let yourself go any further than you have."

I stared at her now in honest amazement. "Eve, I don't mean to be rude, but what if I did? What if I fell madly in love with Mirella? What business is it of yours?"

I had said it as pleasantly as I could, with a smile, but I knew that I was risking offending her. In fact, she didn't react at all. She was thoughtful for a moment, as if I had raised a legitimate point. Then, in a matter-of-fact voice, she gave me her answer. "Because I feel responsible."

"Responsible? Why?"

"I introduced you."

"What's wrong with that? You've introduced me to a lot of people."

"But not to anyone like Mirella. She's different. Very different. And I didn't warn you."

"Warn me? About what?" I asked. "Are you referring to that sick gossip I've been hearing? About Tobias's death?"

She paused, perhaps a bit surprised. She may have thought I was in a state of total ignorance about Mirella. "At least you know about *that*," she said.

"Yes, and I think it's all nonsense. I don't believe a word of it."

"I don't know if I do, either. We have no way of knowing the truth, do we? But there is something else that *is* true," Eve went on, "something in Mirella's past. Almost no one in our set knows about it. Tobias knew, of course," she added. "He learned about it eventually. It seemed to make no difference to him.

"What is it?"

After a moment, she asked, "Have you ever wondered why Mirella is living in this country?"

"Yes, I have—a little. Do *you* know why?"

"Yes. She told me when she first came over here. I got it from her bit by bit. She was only eighteen then, her English was shaky, and it was a little difficult communicating with her. But, because of the horrible thing that had happened, she didn't want to associate with people from her own country. So we became friends and she confided in me."

"What *had* happened?"

"Her mother murdered a man."

I was stunned. "Who?"

"Her lover."

Ordinarily, on hearing so dramatic a statement, I might have automatically responded, "Are you serious?" But I didn't doubt the truth of it. From the first, I had wondered about Mirella's secret. And all along I had sensed that it had to be something as shocking as this.

"When did it happen?" I asked, finally.

"About thirteen years ago," Eve replied. "It was a very famous case in Italy—and the notoriety was more than Mirella could bear. She stayed through the trial. Then she came to this country. She's only been back for short stays since."

"Where did the murder take place?"

"In the Ludovisi palazzo."

I was a bit astonished. "She killed her lover *there?*"

"He lived there," Eve explained. "He worked for Mirella's father. As his secretary, or something like that. Her father felt very close to this man," she went on. "And I guess the shock of the whole thing must have been too much for him. He died a year later."

"How did it happen?" I asked. "I mean—why did her mother do it?"

"I don't really know," she said. "A crime of passion, I suppose. The Contessa fired two bullets into her lover's heart. Then she went to the phone and called the police." She paused uncertainly. "I have a feeling she never did explain why—to the police, to anyone."

"Where is she now? In prison?"

"In a mental institution. She was declared insane."

"God, poor Mirella!" I thought about it for a moment, imagined the pain that must have been with her every day. Such a memory wouldn't go away; such a fact could never be undone. At length, I asked, "What's she like—her mother?"

"Mirella only told me a little bit about her. But we can get some idea from knowing Mirella." Eve looked at me intently. "I think she must be very much like her mother."

Her look was a meaningful one. "Is that meant to be a warning, too?" I asked.

"I'm fond of you, Carl," she said. "And I know you're bright. But you can be as blind as any man." She paused. "As blind as Tobias was."

"Thanks for your concern, Eve," I said. "But Mirella is just a beautiful girl to me. And she doesn't scare me one bit."

Eve shrugged and smiled resignedly, as if she had done her duty and there was nothing more she could say, or felt it necessary to say.

8

When I got home, I went straight to my typewriter and hammered out an outline for my novel. the major events of the book came to me in a rush. My imagination was fired up now. This last revelation had done the trick.

It was what the story had needed, a primal crime in the recent past, laying the shadow of a curse on the family, leaving an indelible stain of blood on the marble floor of the palazzo.

It was gothic. It was dark and horrifying. And it had the ingredients. Sex. Violence. Elemental passion. Mystery.

Actually, when it came to the real-life case, there was even more mystery than before. Eve's sketchy recounting of it had raised as many questions in my mind as it had answered. Perhaps some of these questions were now unanswerable—which didn't really matter to me. As a novelist, I didn't want to have my fancy fettered by too much in the way of fact. Still, the true story of the Count and Countess Ludovisi, and the unfortunate lover-secretary, was now one of the sources that was inspiring my fiction. I knew I should make some effort to learn what I could of it.

Who would know about it? I wondered. Eve had said it was a famous case, so presumably any knowledgeable Italian who had been living in his country at that time would have been familiar with it.

Enrico Sebastiani. He seemed to be my best bet. Enrico was a correspondent for one of the newspapers in Milan. He had resided in New York for twenty years or more, covering the American cultural scene for his Italian readers. But he hadn't lost touch with his native land; I knew he went back home frequently. He had a keen nose for all the New York gossip, and I felt sure that he had kept up with the more notorious scandals in Italy, too.

Enrico was only a casual acquaintance. I didn't even have a phone number for him. But I knew where I probably could find him—at The Lion's Head, the literary saloon on Sheridan Square. In the tradition of the sociable European intellectual, he maintained regular hours there, much as he would have at a favored sidewalk cafe' in Rome or Paris.

Late that evening, around ten, I walked over to The Lion's Head. It was packed, with the crowd, as always, at its thickest around the bar. Enrico usually managed to claim a sliver of the bar. He would stand at an angle to it, in the same unrelinquished spot for a full evening, chatting animatedly with whatever people happened to end up beside him.

This time, though, I didn't see him at the bar or anywhere else. I glanced around for someone to ask about him. Otto Ullman, who was even more of a Lion's Head regular than Enrico, was standing up against a wall, under the framed dust jackets of a couple of forgotten novels, with the thick, evilly glowing stub of a cigar in his mouth. I had never seen Otto without a cigar, and I had never seen him with one that wasn't near its end; it was as if he purchased them in the stub state.

I went over to Otto and asked, "Have you seen Enrico Sebastiani?"

"Not yet," Otto replied. "He should be around."

I bought a bottle of beer and then returned to Otto. He wasn't the most charming person there, and certainly not the most attractive—he was short and squat, with the silted-down bulginess of someone who spends too much time behind a typewriter—but I knew him a little better than anyone else who was in the tavern at that point.

"Are they keeping you busy, Otto?" I asked.

"You better believe it," he said wearily. "I've got to turn in a book at the end of next month. I'm starting it tomorrow."

"A Jennifer?" I asked. Otto was a specialist in romantic fiction, and he wrote most of his novels under female pseudonyms. I couldn't remember any of them, only that one had "Jennifer" as the first name.

"Nah, this isn't a Jennifer," Otto said. "Jennifer writes the gothics. This is a bodice-ripper. Jennifer is too much of a lady to write this kind of garbage. This is a Rhoda."

I laughed, even though I wasn't sure he meant it as a joke. And it was, in fact, more appalling to me than funny. Otto worked for a packager, and he cranked out a half dozen or so junk novels every year for the mass paperback market. It was the fate, I feared, that awaited me, if I couldn't get my creative act together.

"What about you, Carl?" he asked. "Finishing up another book?"

"Starting one. Something that should interest you," I added. "It's sort of a gothic."

"A gothic?" Otto looked at me quizzically. "You?"

"Well, I'm not sure," I admitted. "How do you know when a book is a gothic?"

"Is there a large, spooky house with a single lit window?"

"No, But there's a palazzo."

"An Italian gothic? Interesting." He puffed on his cigar thoughtfully. "Do you have a timid young woman who might be in peril?"

"I have a timid man who *is* in peril."

"Then it's not a gothic," Otto said flatly. "It's got to be a woman."

"Why can't there be gothics for timid men?" I asked.

"Great!" he said, with a laugh. "You're creating a new genre."

I caught sight of Enrico Sebastiani. He had just entered and was standing by the end of the bar, taking in the scene. He was a dapper, bearded little man in soft tweeds, with a cravat neatly knotted at his throat.

I excused myself and went over to Enrico. "How are you, Enrico?"

"Fine, Carl," he said. "How's the world treating you?" Enrico was fond of using American colloquial expressions, though he didn't seem to realize when they had reached the cliché point.

"I'm not complaining," I replied, with equal freshness. "Let me buy you a drink. I want to talk to you about something."

Enrico acquiesced readily. As an international journalist, he was doubtless accustomed to having people, for whatever motivation, try to plant items with him. In this case, though he didn't realize it yet, I wanted to extract information from *him*.

We went into the other room and sat at a small table in the far corner; it was the closest we could get to privacy. We ordered our drinks. Then, when the waitress departed, Enrico looked at me questioningly.

"What's up?" he asked.

"Well," I began, "I've gotten to know an Italian girl. Maybe you know her, too. Mirella Ludovisi?"

"Mirella? Sure. She's a knockout," he said appreciatively.

"Is she a friend?" I asked uncertainly.

"No, not a friend. But she's one of the Italian colony here. We all know each other." He cocked his head to one side and eyed me curiously. "Why are you asking about her?"

"We're working on a project together. Some scholarly papers she's inherited."

This was a dead issue with me, of course, but I was prepared to use the Walling manuscript as an excuse for my interest in her. Enrico, however, didn't seem to pick up on this. He said nothing, but simply waited politely for me to go on. It was possible, I realized, that he didn't know the tragic story of Mirella's fiancé.

"Someone told me what happened in her family," I went on. "Her mother murdering her lover. You know about that?"

"Yes."

"It was a real shocker when I heard it."

He nodded. "A terrible thing."

"I realize what a painful subject it must be for her. So I can't ask her about it. But if I'm going to be working closely with her, I feel I should know something more about it."

"Why?"

"To satisfy my curiosity, I guess."

Enrico shrugged and said, "I don't know how much *I* can tell you."

"Well, do you know anything about her parents? Her father, for instance?"

"Only a little—I never met the man. His name was Vittorio Ludovisi. From what I understand, he was a typical specimen of his class."

"Which means what?"

"A parasite."

I hadn't known anything about Enrico's political beliefs. But apparently he was somewhat left-wing—when it came to his own country, anyway.

"He was in the Italian air force, wasn't he?"

Enrico nodded. "During the war. He commanded a fighter squadron. It was the only useful thing he ever did." With a thin smile, he added, "If you call fighting for Mussolini a useful thing."

"Was he a Fascist?" I asked.

"All the nobility were Fascists. Of course, now they say they were in the Resistance—every last one of them. But then it was the Second Roman Empire, and they were conquerors again." He laughed. "You saw what marvelous warriors they turned out to be."

"How old was Ludovisi at the time of the murder?"

"Near sixty."

"The lover was young, I suppose?"

"He wasn't a boy. But, yes, he was younger. In his early forties, I think."

"And he was working as a secretary?"

"His position was more exalted than that. He was a literary man who was down on his luck. He was working with Ludovisi on that history he was writing—as an editor and researcher."

"What about Mirella's mother?" I asked. "The Contessa. Was she born an aristocrat, too?"

"Of course," Enrico said. "More than that. She was born a Ludovisi."

"The same family?"

"A second cousin. Those people," he said, shaking his head disgustedly, "they are so inbred, it's a wonder they don't all have harelips. As it is, many of them are crazy. The Contessa is no big exception."

"Do you know *why* she killed her lover?"

"I just said it. She's crazy."

"Being crazy isn't enough by itself to make someone kill."

"For *those* people, it's enough," he said emphatically. "They all have murder in their hearts."

"I think you're making a political statement, Enrico," I commented mildly, "not a statement of fact."

"You don't think so? What is a nobleman?" he asked rhetorically. "Someone who had a brute of an ancestor who could swing a sword or a battle-axe more ferociously, kill more people that the other brutes. And so the king or the duke rewarded him by giving him some land, some peasants, and a title. And what would happen when one of these noble brutes married the child of another noble brute? When the brutes kept intermarrying, through the generations, pooling their genes? After several centuries, what would you get? A humanist? No. A homicidal maniac!"

"Okay," I said, "maybe you're right." I didn't want to have to argue with him about his cockeyed theory. I had no stake in the issue. It was class war to Enrico, just a story background to me. "But we're not living in the Middle Ages now. And those people—people like the Ludovisi—aren't swinging swords and battle-axes these days. Land and money is what they're all about."

"Land? Money?" He looked at me perplexedly, as if I had raised an irrelevant point. "The Ludovisi have no money."

"They don't?" This was something of a surprise to me. "But they have that palazzo."

"Yes, they have their palazzo, and I'm sure Mirella would never give it up. But a big old building like that can be like an albatross. Do you think we have no property taxes in Italy?"

"But what about all the land they own? The rents coming in?"

"They may have two or three small farms left. But no more than that. The Contessa's trial ruined them. Most of the land had to be sold to pay the legal costs."

I thought about this for a moment. Mirella had given me a very different impression. But her descriptions of the idyllic, feudal life, of the peasants coming by to give the Ludovisi the first fruits of their crops, might have applied to her childhood only, to a world that was forever gone for her.

Still, I couldn't be sure that Enrico wasn't exaggerating. "There was enough money to put Mirella through Sarah Lawrence," I pointed out. "And that's one of the most expensive schools in this country."

"Yes, but that was about the last of it. Since then, Mirella has had a very hard time."

"Well," I said, "she's no longer having a hard time."

"I heard." Enrico gave me an inquiring look. "I heard that the man she was going to marry left her some money. Is it true?"

"Yes, it's true."

"A lot?"

"Quite a lot."

"Good for her!" he said, nodding approvingly. "I remember there were times when that girl had nothing. She'd keep up the front, the elegant front. But she'd have nothing at all. She wasn't raised to work like other people. So she'd stay in that one room she lived in over on the West Side, and just wait for the birds to feed her."

"*Did* the birds feed her?"

"Not exactly. But, sooner or later, a man would come along and take care of her for a while." He shrugged. "A girl that beautiful doesn't really starve, does she? Mirella has always had some man."

His worldly smile annoyed me, and his words had an unpleasant ring for me. It wasn't what I wanted to hear about Mirella.

Still, I told myself, I shouldn't be naive. If I was to do my work properly, I had to be clear-eyed about the woman. I thought back to her wanton gesture, the offering of her bare breast to me. The suggestion of the courtesan about it, I realized now, had not been accidental.

And I was beginning to understand the significance of the Walling inheritance to her. It had been no meaningless windfall, riches descending on someone who was already rich. Mirella had desperately needed that fortune from the beginning. This put a different light on the situation. It made all of her professions of her love for Tobias suspect.

But then, I reminded myself, genuine love and personal profit could coincide. There was no reason to be cynical about it. I had to give Mirella the benefit of the doubt.

Enrico was looking thoughtful now. "This money she inherited," he asked, finally, "it was a great deal? As much as a million, maybe?"

"Many millions," I replied.

He let out his breath slowly, an impressed sigh. "Then Mirella has turned out to be lucky, after all."

"Lucky? With her father dead and her mother in an insane asylum?"

"Not now," he said.

"What do you mean—not now?"

"The Contessa is no longer in the institution."

"They released her?"

"No. She escaped. Last year."

I stared at him. "Then where is she now?"

"No one knows," he said. "No one knows where she is."

9

I soon made another discovery about Mirella. She was a jogger.

Perhaps it shouldn't have surprised me. A young woman with her figure was bound to do something physical to maintain it. Still, my image of her had been as a housebound beauty, reclining languidly in her living room, surrounded by Persian art, in an atmosphere heavy with the fragrance of cut flowers. I hadn't imagined her in sweat pants and Adidas, trotting along the East River in the early morning hours.

Not only did I now have to imagine it, but one morning she persuaded me to share this gruesome exercise with her.

Mirella had been fretting about my health. There was nothing wrong with it so far as I could tell. But it worried her that I still smoked cigarettes, had an occasional coughing fit, and hadn't seen a doctor in years. Also, it seemed, I was the one who struck *her* as unwholesome and shut-in, as someone who didn't get out into the open air nearly enough.

I had had more than my share of maternal talking-tos in my time with Denny. It was in character for Denny; she had been the captain of her girls' school basketball team, and she came from an Illinois family of tough old birds who thought it shameful to die before ninety. But it puzzled me a little that the exotic Mirella would take the same tack with me. I was functioning, after all; I wasn't a broken-down wreck.

She explained it simply. "Remember," she said, "I've lost the men I've loved." She left the thought unspoken that she didn't want to lose me, too.

And so, on a nippy spring morning, I jogged down the path by the river, side by side with Mirella. There wasn't much conversation; it was all I could do just to breathe. But, from time to time, she would glance at me and smile, as if she were pleased I was managing so nicely—or perhaps pleased with herself that she had done this terrific thing for me.

After a while, it began to seem almost pleasurable. It was rather sociable on that path: we had plenty of company and Mirella would occasionally raise her hand in greeting as one of the regulars passed by, going in the other direction. Her running motion was smooth and graceful and there was an esthetic satisfaction to be had in harmonizing my movement with hers. It was as healthy and pure an activity as a couple could share, an all-American kind of activity, and, while we were jogging by the river, with barges and excursion boats cruising serenely nearby, it was impossible to give thought to dark, violent deeds in distant lands or mad, murderous mothers.

We went a mile down the path and then a mile back to our starting point. I lasted the full course, incurring only a moderate pain in my chest. I was even able to pull off a finishing kick at the end. I had been something of a flash in my youth and I wasn't going to let a girl finish ahead of me.

Afterward, we walked over to Second Avenue, where Mirella gave me a peck on the cheek and left me to do some shopping. She was going up to East Eighty-sixth Street to buy what was needed for the feast she was to prepare for me the next evening. It would be our first dinner together at her house. And, she had hinted, the beginning of other things as well.

I looked around for a cab. But it was the morning rush hour and there was no free one in sight. I started down the avenue, expecting that an empty cab would come by eventually. My legs were aching, the old sweatshirt I was wearing wasn't providing sufficient warmth, and I hoped I wouldn't have to walk far.

I didn't have much luck, though. After going three or four blocks, I was ready to give up and take a subway. But I heard a familiar voice crying out behind me, "Carl! Carl!"

I stopped and turned. Denny was hurrying after me—running, actually—though the second after I turned, she slowed to a walk, not wanting to seem *too* eager to catch up with me, I supposed.

I wasn't too surprised to see her. Denny lived in that neighborhood, and I had just passed her cross street. I knew that, when the weather was decent, she usually walked down to the bus that went crosstown to her place of work, a television studio in the West Sixties. I assumed that was what she was doing now, since she was carrying her tote bag, which was usually crammed with research material.

When she came up to me, Denny stammered nervously for an instant, "What—?" and then got the question out. "What are *you* doing here?" She liked to think of me as a chronic Villager who, as the old gag line had it, got nosebleeds north of Fourteenth Street.

"Can't you tell? I've been working out," I said, patting my damp sweatshirt. "Jogging by the river."

She looked incredulous. "You?"

I shrugged. "When you reach a certain age—" The vigorous exercise had temporarily rid me of the need to smoke. But now, suddenly confronted by Denny, I unthinkingly took out my pack of cigarettes.

"You haven't given up smoking, I see," she said, in the tone of disapproval I remembered so well.

I sheepishly put the cigarettes back into my pants pocket. "You can't get too healthy too fast," I said. "It isn't good for your system."

She laughed. Then we just looked at each other for a moment.

Denny was wearing a belted raincoat and I knew that there was a collapsible umbrella in her tote bag; if there was so much as one cloud in the sky, she was fearful of rain. It wasn't that she minded getting wet; she was vain of her thick, reddish-blond hair. She felt that nature was constantly conspiring to take the curl out of it.

"Let's have some coffee," she said.

"Won't you be late to work?"

"I've some time yet. Anyway, it's a slow morning."

"I didn't know there *was* such a thing in television," I said. "But okay."

There was a little diner on the corner up ahead. We went into it and settled in a booth at the rear, ordering Danish pastries with our coffee to justify taking up the space.

Our orders came promptly. I took a sip of coffee, but kept my eyes on Denny, searching for any subtle, telltale signs of change in her. She seemed more freckled than I remembered. Of course, the freckles might all have been there before; when you're close to someone it's the kind of thing you stop seeing. She seemed more than merely pretty to me now, downright gorgeous. But then her beauty might have been something else I had grown blind to. Her skin was totally clear, not a blemish anywhere. Her breakouts, as I remembered, had happened when she was suffering either from work tension or sexual neglect. It made me uneasy to see her complexion so flawless.

"How's the writing going?" she asked.

"I've started another book."

"Oh, good. Can you tell me about it?"

"I'd rather not." *This* book was one I was particularly reluctant to discuss with Denny. "So, what's been happening with you?" I asked.

"The same. Work," she said. "We've got some exciting shows coming up."

"Who have you landed this time? Warren Beatty? Gore Vidal?"

The sarcasm had come into my voice unintentionally, as a habit reflex. After all, I had no right to make an issue of it now; her obsession with celebrities was no longer my concern. But it had been one of several irritants in our relationship. Her fascination with the famous went beyond the understandable requirements of her job; it was a fixation that had been preserved unchanged from her childhood. It seemed incongruous, since Denise McLaughlin was something of a figure in the television world. She didn't do the actual booking of the guests on her talk show, but press agents, who wanted to touch all bases, courted her, too. You would have thought she might have been, if not jaded, then at least a bit weary of the hype. But she remained, at heart, the excited little hick girl with her nose pressed against the window.

It was a harmless trait, admittedly, but it had sometimes rubbed my vanity the wrong way. You don't always want to hear the woman you love burble happily about having spent an hour with Norman

Mailer; not if you yourself are a considerably dimmer light in the literary firmament, a speck of the thirty-second magnitude, the sort that doesn't get invited to talk shows.

Denny's face had clouded; evidently, she was picking up the old, familiar vibrations from me. So, instead of answering my question, she said, "Let's not talk about my work."

"Okay, let's not," I said. "Let's talk about something else. Tell me about your social life."

"What do you want to know? Who I'm seeing?"

I thought about it for a moment. "No," I replied.

We fell silent. It wasn't an awkward silence, not from my point of view, anyway. I was enjoying simply being with her, sitting this close to her, watching the play of expression on her face. It was hard to remember now why I had decided that life would be easier without her. Or even if I was the one who had decided it. That last quarrel had been a messy business, with both of us saying things we would have been wiser not to say, saying them simultaneously, with equal volume, equal anger.

The issue with her had been so clear-cut and normal as to be banal. She was nearing thirty-five and she wanted to be married. Despite my unpleasant past experience of it, I had nothing against marriage as such. But I told her that I found marriage unromantic and, for the time being, I wanted to keep our affair romantic.

That was as false as it was corny. The plain truth was that I was unhappy. Unhappy with my career, with my creative stagnation, with my life as a whole. And the worse I felt about myself, the less good I felt about Denny.

At length, Denny said, "Phil and Nancy have asked about you."

"Oh? How are they?"

"Fine. Phil's got a great new job."

"Yeah?" I responded, with no surprise. Phil was in advertising and he got a great new job every two years. "Where'd he go?"

"Ogilvy."

"More money?"

"A lot more money. And they're giving him some of the top accounts."

"Well, terrific."

"They say they miss you."

"I'll give them a call sometime," I said.

I didn't really intend to. At that point, it would have seemed artificial to make contact with Phil and Nancy, or with any of the other friends I had lost touch with. It was sad, but that was the way it was. As after a divorce, our friends had chosen between us. Not too surprisingly, it had been Denny, ten to one.

We were silent again. Then Denny said, "I called you last week."

"You did? Why?"

"I just had an urge to talk to you."

She had said it with a shrug, but she wasn't looking at me now. She tore off a little piece of her napkin and started working it into a ball between her thumb and index finger. It was a nervous habit of hers—I had seen her do it many times—and I don't think she was ever actually aware that she was doing it.

"Wasn't my answering machine working?" I asked.

"Oh, sure. I don't like talking to machines."

I remembered it now, that particular minute of silence on the tape. It had been the only hang-up-without-a-message on my machine that week. "Oh, yeah. That must have been the night I went out to the theater."

Her fingers, pinching the bit of paper, went still, and she looked at me directly. "With that Italian woman?"

"Oh, you know?"

"Someone told me."

"Okay, then, yes. I was with Mirella."

"Your new friend?"

"We're seeing each other," I said casually.

I wasn't trying to make anything of it. But, at the same time, I was taking a certain satisfaction in Denny's very obvious jealousy.

"Isn't she supposed to be a duchess or something?" she asked.

"A Countess."

"Does she want to make *you* a Count?"

"I don't think it's legal."

Denny just looked grim for a moment. "Well," she said, "it's none of my business."

"No. Any more than the men you're seeing are *my* business."

With that point established, we both turned to our Danish pastries and nibbled for a few moments. Denny's expression had softened, as if she had, indeed, put unpleasant thoughts behind here.

"You know, Carl," she said, finally, "there's no reason for us to be total strangers for the rest of our lives."

"No reason at all," I agreed.

"We can still get together and talk sometimes. Like we're doing now."

"It's nice," I said.

Denny paused. It was a moment of hesitation, I sensed, a moment of nerving herself. "Phil and Nancy are having a party tomorrow night," she said. "Why don't you come with me? They're dying to see you again."

"I'd love to," I said.

I meant it. It struck me as a wonderful idea, a way of wiping out the months of loneliness in one enjoyable evening. It would restore some old friendships. Also, it might begin to undo my stupidity in letting Denny slip away from me—lovely, adorable Denny, who had been guilty of nothing more than wanting to be with me forever.

But then I remembered Mirella. I was supposed to have dinner at her house the next evening. It was to be the significant evening, the evening of consummation.

Of course, I could try to get Mirella to change it to another night. But that would risk offending her, risk our entire relationship. And I didn't want to do that, now that I was so close to having her, possessing her, not only her physical being but the mystery of her.

It wasn't just desire. There was my book. I couldn't forget my book.

"Unfortunately," I went on, "I can't do it. I'm having dinner with someone."

Denny's face turned cold. "With that woman?"

"Yes."

It vanished then. With the ducking of Denny's head, it was gone: the opening she had offered me, the chance to return to some degree of happiness.

But she didn't understand. I had an idea and I had to live it out. Happiness could wait.

10

The silver candlesticks, the crystal goblets, the creamy china with its gold-inlay pattern, all seemed to come from another age. I imagined that these elegant objects had been in the Ludovisi family for some time, and that Mirella had carried them about with her over the years, as part of a small hoard of cherished household items that she would someday bring to a marriage.

As I sat in the flickering candlelight, at a table set as it would have been for princes, I found it hard to believe that East Eighty-fourth Street was only a few yards away. We were in a separate dining room with a door that had been closed, so we didn't hear the street noises. And the house itself was totally silent. It was the maid's night off and the two of us were alone. Mirella had prepared the dinner herself.

She had done a spectacular job. A tomato bisque was followed by linguini with a butter-and-cheese sauce. And then came thin slices of veal, bathed in creamy lemon sauce. The vegetables, spinach and zucchini, had been delicately sautéed in olive oil. The process had been terminated at just the right moment, with the perfect sense of timing that only Northern Italian cooks seem to have.

I lost myself in the pleasures of eating and, for a few minutes, I almost forgot why I was there. This dinner seemed to be enough of an event in itself. But it wasn't likely that I would forget the real purpose of the evening—not with Mirella looking so seductively beautiful.

She had put me at the head of the table and she was sitting on my left; fairly close, so that the scent of her perfume was constantly in my nostrils. She was wearing a light-blue filmy dress—not see-through, exactly, but with enough transparency that I could discern she had nothing on underneath. Her hair was loose, almost wild, and it fell forward onto her cheek when she leaned forward to refill my wineglass.

She did this several times, and the last time I stopped her. Too much wine and I wouldn't be able to perform as a man—if that, indeed, was to be the climax of this evening.

We went on to our coffee. But we weren't, as it turned out, through with drinking. When we were half finished with our cups of espresso, Mirella left the dining room and then returned with an opened bottle of some other kind of wine. It was a dusty old bottle that had no label on it.

"This is from our cellar in Ferrara," she said. "I still have a few bottles left."

She refilled my glass from this bottle. I knew too little about wine to ask any intelligent question. I simply inquired, "What is it?"

"It's a wine from my region," she replied. "From a little vineyard we once owned. Tell me if you like it."

I took a swallow of it. It was full-flavored, and it seemed to have an immediate headiness to it. There was a heavy earthiness that I had sometimes found in fine old wines, a taste that made me think of reopened graves.

"Very nice," I said. I noticed that her glass was still empty. "Aren't you having some, too?"

Mirella filled her glass and took a very small sip of the wine. She smiled and said, "It reminds me of home."

This sounded like the conversational lead-in I had been waiting for. I had decided that I would ask her about the murder of her mother's lover, ask her about it directly. But until now she had made no reference to her past, to Ferrara, and I had had no opportunity to set up my question.

"It reminds you of happy things?" I asked.

"Of course. Happy things."

"But some of your memories are *not* happy."

"No, they are not all happy."

I sat back and took another swallow of the wine. Then I said, "Mirella, you told me once that there'd been a tragedy in your family. You said you couldn't tell me about it. You were afraid to."

She was gazing at me steadily now. "Yes," she said, and waited.

As I paused, I wondered about my timing. I could be destroying this evening, with all of its possibilities, then and there. Still, from some gentlemanly instinct, I felt I should get it out in the open early, before we made love rather than after.

"I know about it now," I said.

"Oh? Someone has talked to you?"

I didn't want to implicate Eve Lukas. So I said, "An Italian journalist mentioned it to me."

"Who?"

"No one you're acquainted with," I lied. I thought it best to keep Enrico out of it, too.

"Very well," she said calmly. "Now you know." After a moment, she added, "I would have told you eventually."

"Maybe it's just as well I learned about it this way. I mean, it must be painful for you to talk about it."

"Oh, I can talk about it. It was a long time ago."

That was true of the murder itself. But, if Enrico had informed me correctly, her mother had escaped from the mental institution as recently as the previous year. However, I had decided that I wouldn't bring up this fact with Mirella. I remembered her strange, tense response when I had first asked her about her mother. I sensed that, even now, no matter how ready she was to be candid about some aspects of the story, she would still be unwilling to discuss her mother's present circumstances. And, for all I knew, her answer at the time—that the Contessa was in China with her diplomat brother— might have been the truth.

"I'm not asking you to talk about it," I said. "But I'm glad I know. It helps me to understand you—the sadness in you. That event that happened, though"—I found I couldn't use a word like "murder" to her face—"that kind of thing I can never understand."

"Why can't you understand it?" she asked.

"Well—to take someone's life. What could justify doing that? Was this man so bad?"

"Gianfranco? No, he wasn't bad. He was very nice. Very sensitive. You would have liked him."

"Did you know him well?"

"Of course. He lived with us. I knew him very well." With a little smile that suggested the shyness of a teenage girl, she added, "I had a crush on him."

"Then why did your mother do it?" I asked. "Why did she kill him?"

She seemed a bit surprised that I was even asking the question. It was as if, to her, it was a question that could have only one answer.

"He wanted to leave," she said simply.

"And your mother wasn't willing to give him up?"

"Not in that way."

"What way?" I paused, then ventured, "Was there another woman?"

"Yes."

"He wanted to go off with this other woman?"

"Worse than that. He wanted to marry her. My mother would not have minded if he had just had an affair. But he wanted to marry this woman."

"And she was so possessive about him that she killed him?"

Mirella looked at me impassively for a moment. "He belonged with us," she said.

Something in her tone made me uneasy. "But you didn't *own* him," I said.

"My father had taken in Gianfranco when he was nothing—a starving writer who couldn't sell anything. He couldn't leave us like that—suddenly—just for a woman. It would not have been fair to my mother—or to my father."

"Buy your father didn't know about Gianfranco being your mother's lover, did he?"

"Yes," she said, "of course he did. It didn't matter to him. He was fond of Gianfranco."

"Now, wait a minute!" This sophistication—or decadence—was more than I could accept all at once. "You say that your father didn't object to your mother having a lover. And that your mother wouldn't have minded if Gianfranco had had an affair with another woman. Well, it sounds as if they were very open-minded—your mother and your father both. So, why did your mother have that fit of jealousy?"

76

"It wasn't jealousy," she replied. "I told you, Gianfranco wanted to *marry* this woman. She couldn't let him do it. She couldn't let him shame her like that."

Mirella was explaining this in a reasonable way, as if, rather than speculating on a mad act of violence, she was giving a sensible motivation for a plausible action. Responding as much to her tone as to what she was saying, I murmured, "I don't understand."

"No, Carl," she said, "I know you don't. To understand, you would have to understand the Italians—the Italians of my class, anyway. To us, the family is sacred, and the relationships within a family are sacred. Gianfranco had become one of our family. And it was no secret. Ferrara is a small place. It was known that he was my mother's lover—and it was accepted. But what Gianfranco wanted to do showed no respect. He wanted to *marry* this woman, so that my mother would have been publicly rejected—for the whole world to see. That would have humiliated her. That would have dishonored her. She couldn't deal with that." With a shrug, she concluded, "You know what she did."

A wave of dizziness hit me suddenly. I leaned back in my chair and closed my eyes for a moment.

When I opened them again, I saw that Mirella was looking at me intently. "Are you all right?" she asked.

"The wine seems to be getting to me," I said.

She took the half-empty glass from my hand. She put it down beside her own, which was still full; she hadn't touched her wine after the first sip.

"Enough of this talk," she said. "Let's go upstairs."

We rose. I looked at her uncertainly, a bit stupidly perhaps, but she took me by the hand and led me out of the dining room. We went up the stairway to the next floor. The dizziness had vanished, but I was a little unsteady going up the stairs. I was starting to wonder about it. Had there been something in that last dusty bottle? Three or four glasses of wine didn't usually have much effect on me.

When we reached the top of the stairs, we didn't, as I expected, turn to the left to go toward her bedroom. Instead Mirella turned right and we went to a room that was at the opposite end of the hallway. She opened the door, entered the room, and I followed her in.

It was another bedroom, but much smaller than the master bedroom, and plainer, barely furnished. There was a double bed, with the covers turned down, a dresser topped by a mirror, a single straight-backed chair, a table with a shaded lamp on it that was providing the only illumination, and that was all.

"This is *your* room," Mirella said.

I didn't quite know what she meant by this, whether she was saying that this room was for my exclusive use or indicating that the other private rooms in the house, including her own, were out of bounds for me. Also, there was a suggestion of captivity about it. It was accidental, I was sure, but it made me uneasy.

Mirella pulled her dress up over her head, tossed it aside, and stood in the center of the room, naked. She was as perfect as I had imagined. Hastily and awkwardly, I undressed, not bothering to be neat about it, leaving my clothes in a heap on the floor. In a matter of seconds, I too, was naked. I advanced toward her.

She didn't receive my kiss on her mouth but averted her head so that I was pressing my lips against her cheek and neck. I had her in my arms and I was already erect. If it hadn't been for the difference in our heights, I could have entered her then and there.

"Let's look at ourselves," she said.

She drew me a step closer to the dresser and turned. We both looked at our reflections in the wood-framed mirror. Her reflection smiled; she seemed pleased with what she was seeing. In the dim light our faces had softened, transformed. Mirella's beauty had taken on a smokiness, the changeableness of something seen in a mist. I didn't like my features any better than I usually did—the short nose with the broad nostrils, the too-thin mouth, still displeased me— but I was looking younger, more romantic, a proper partner for this lovely creature.

She went over to the bed and sat on the edge of it. I followed and sat beside her. She took my hand, but didn't look up at me.

Then the dizziness hit me again. I released her hand, lay back on the bed, full-length, and waited for it to pass.

But my desire hadn't abated. If anything, it had increased. My erection remained, painfully insistent. I was beginning to think that if my wine had, in fact, been doctored, it might have been with an aphrodisiac. Certainly, as I blearily regarded Mirella, sitting motionless beside me, took in the side view of her, gazed at her breasts, thrusting outward with the large red nipples firm and distended, I wanted her more than I had ever wanted any woman.

She still wasn't looking at me, but a little smile had come onto her lips. "Are you going to sodomize me?" she asked.

The question startled me. Also, I was unsure as to what she meant, since "sodomy" is a term that covers a variety of practices. "You mean—in the rear?" I asked.

"Yes."

"Why do you think I'd do that?"

"It's in your book," she said.

The gamiest scene in my novel, I remembered now, had described the buggering of my heroine by a cruel mogul. I had had her enjoy every painful moment of it. But that was tawdry commercialism; it wasn't supposed to be taken as self-revelation on my part.

"Mirella," I said, "what I write and what I do are very different things."

She turned her head and looked at me. The small, secret smile was still there, and I could tell she didn't really believe me. "That was a very graphic scene," she said. "I read it several times."

I laughed suddenly, as I was struck by the absurdity of it. Here I had been pursuing this dark, mysterious beauty to live out a gothic romance with her, and this same mysterious beauty, I suspected now, was a horny lady who wanted *me* because I had turned her on with a dirty book!

Her face darkened. "Why are you laughing?"

"Oh, nothing." I put my hand on her thigh and stroked it lightly. "Let's not talk about literature any more."

79

The touch of my hand on her thigh seemed to trigger something in her. A shudder went through her. She let out a whimper and, in a sudden, convulsive movement, drew her legs up onto the bed and bent over me. I started to lift myself up to embrace her, but she pressed me back down onto the mattress. Then she closed her hand around my penis and straddled me.

I waited for us to join. but it didn't happen. In a quick, steady rhythm, she rose up and down on the tip of my penis, chafing herself with it, crying out excitedly with each instant of friction. I tried to force myself upward to penetrate her. But she griped me firmly; I was fixed in place. Her cries ascended in pitch and she climaxed. She let go of me and threw herself face down on the bed.

I lay there throbbing, arching with unreleased tension. I was confused and angry. I felt that I had been degraded, contemptuously reduced to an implement, an object for masturbation. I couldn't leave it that way.

I looked at Mirella, lying on her stomach beside me. The heaving of her back was gradually subsiding as she came down from her orgasm. Her extended legs were slightly angled and, where the thighs began to separate, I saw the glistening lips, the entryway that had been denied me. It was easily accessible now.

I rolled over and drove myself into her. She screamed, a harsh cry that didn't sound human but like the screech of a cat being violated. She struggled at first, but I grabbed her hair at the base of her scalp and twisted it, and soon she went still. I didn't take long; I came even more rapidly than she had.

I lay on her, spent, for a few moments. Then I separated myself from her, eased onto my side, and peered into her face.

Mirella's eyes were staring at me and her face was contorted with rage. Her hand came up swiftly and clawed at my cheek.

I let out a little cry of pain, sat up quickly, and put a hand to my scratched face. When I took my hand away, I saw that there was a pink wetness on my fingers.

I looked at her again. Mirella was sitting up and she was smiling— an excited, triumphant smile. She laughed when she saw my expression.

I realized now that all of this, right up to the final moment of drawn blood, had been as she had wanted it to be.

Suddenly, I was overcome with an immense drowsiness. This was beyond being a dizzy spell. It was as if, with my last ounce of energy expended, I had nothing left to keep myself awake. I was sinking helplessly into unconsciousness.

I lay back and closed my eyes. I opened them again just once, when I was already almost asleep. Mirella was adjusting the blankets around my shoulders. She leaned forward and kissed me lightly on the lips. It was the first time she had kissed me that evening.

It was a deep but troubled sleep. I don't know if I actually dreamed in any coherent way. But, even in my unconscious state, I was aware that this wasn't a natural sleep. I was slowly falling, was being pulled down against my will into frightening depths. Something in me was warning me, was telling me I must surface, get free. But I was powerless. As I fell, I clawed at a void.

I did awaken briefly. I don't know how much time had passed, but the room was dark and the only light was coming from the hall, through the open doorway. I was vaguely aware that it was the opening of the door that had woken me up.

My eyelids were so heavy that I could part them only a crack. But I could see that two female figures were standing in the doorway, watching me. They were too shadowy for me to make out their faces. I knew that one of them was Mirella. The other woman was taller and heavier.

The door closed and now it was totally dark. I struggled to stay awake, to try to understand what was happening. I heard the women talking in the hall. I recognized Mirella's voice. The other voice was deeper, as musical as Mirella's but with a gravity and a quietness to it.

I strained to hear what they were saying, but it was useless. They were speaking in Italian.

And then the sleep reclaimed me. I was falling again, falling into nothingness.

PART TWO

11

I took the completed page out of my typewriter, added it to the previous one, and read over the section I had just written:

Raymond started to get out of the car, then stopped himself. Paolo, with insectile swiftness, had flown out from behind the steering wheel and was coming around to open the door for him. Raymond didn't want to violate an Italian servant's sense of decorum, and he sat still until the door was opened. Then he emerged into the fierce sunlight.

He looked up at the facade of the palazzo. It was Cinquecento, he saw. The golden age of Ferrara. The golden age that had been the beginning of decadence.

Raymond was being awfully quick, I realized. He was a novelist, nothing more, and yet I was showing him here to be so expert in Italian architecture that he could nail down the period of a building in an instant. I was not, however, the first author to be guilty of such an implausibility. The protagonists of novels were frequently invested with vast stores of improbable erudition. It was a way of making the expository points crisply.

In actuality, of course, Raymond would have been as ignorant as I was, and equally at a loss to describe the facade of a Ferrarese palazzo unless he was looking directly at one. At this point it so happened that he was—and, even after some preliminary research in the library, I wasn't sure what he was seeing.

I had studied photographs of the monumental piles that had belonged to the great dukes and princes. But I still didn't have a clear idea what an ordinary, human-scale palazzo looked like. I made a mental note to ask Mirella to show me pictures of the Ludovisi house.

Paolo took Raymond's luggage out of the car. They entered the palazzo. Raymond was expecting to find Isabella inside, waiting for him. But the large, murky main hall was empty. Arches led into smaller rooms that adjoined the main hall, but they, too, seemed empty. Here there was no sense of the bustling life that animated the surrounding streets. It was hard to believe that, just on the other side of the oakwood front door, sleek Italian youths were puttering by on motor bikes. Within these walls it was still as a museum after closing time. Or as a mausoleum.

Paolo had paused to let Raymond look around. But the manservant said nothing, remaining as silent as he had been from the time he had picked up Raymond at the train station. He knew some English; he had revealed as much when he had introduced himself. But he was a dignified little man, with graying temples and the sad face of one who knew his limits, and perhaps he didn't want to attempt a conversation in a language he didn't know well enough.

"Andiamo, signor," *Paolo said.*

I made a check in the margin to remind myself to look up the spelling of the words in my Italian-English dictionary. That little phrase was about as much Italian as I was ready to risk. My knowledge of the language didn't go too far beyond it.

They walked on and crossed an interior courtyard. The suddenness of the sunlight was startling, as was the heavy fragrance of the roses that were in full bloom around them. Then they were in the dark interior again. Paolo stopped to open the door of a room. He stepped back and let Raymond enter it first.

It was a large bedchamber. The walls consisted of dark wood panels, with patterns carved in them. Glancing up, Raymond saw that the ceiling was painted with a swirling arabesque of flowers.

A stout, middle-aged maid was putting the finishing touches on the bedchamber. Paolo set down the luggage beside the bed and said something in Italian to the maid. She responded with a short, rapid burst of speech, smiled at Raymond, and left.

Paolo turned to him. "The Marchesa will be with you soon," he said. Then, with a little bow, he disappeared.

Raymond was left alone, with the title still resonating oddly in his ear. It was such a grand sounding appellation for the slip of a girl he had known simply as Isabella in New York.

But, of course, in this stately palace, it was her right and proper title. And it was he who was the oddity. The American intruder who had come to steal away the mistress. The barbarian.

He would have to adjust, he realized. And he would have to be careful. The serenity of his surroundings didn't deceive him. He sensed an underlying menace. It was an intangible menace, but it might have, for all he knew, a concrete form, too. There might be dungeons just beneath his feet, or subterranean natural caverns with bloody histories.

And he sensed that he was closer—much closer now—to the heart of Isabella's mystery. That dark, unspeakable crime she had hinted at, the horror that had laid a shadow on her, that haunted her day and night.

Suddenly a wooden panel separated from the rest of the wall and swung backward. It was a hidden door. Isabella appeared in the doorway. She was wearing a long, white dress and her dark hair was loose around her shoulders.

"I am so glad you're here," she said breathlessly.

That was as far as I had gone.

I crossed out "breathlessly," then studied the last few sentences. Isabella's line exactly duplicated Mirella's first words to me at the East Eighty-fourth Street house. But that hidden door might be a little hokey, I thought. Wouldn't it be more logical for Isabella to enter from the doorway that Paolo and the maid had just passed through?

No, I decided, if there were a hidden door, Isabella would use it. Like her prototype, Mirella, she would call upon the symbols of mystery even in the midst of the most painful real-life tragedy. It was an observance of rituals, with the rituals of story having the same force as the rituals of religion. When one is born to fulfill a role, the distinction between the two fades.

Still, symbols and dramatic gestures in themselves couldn't be enough to give substance to this novel. I didn't want this to become some billowing fog of a book, all atmosphere and suggestion, without the solid ground of actuality anywhere. A real American had spent the last weeks of his life in a real palazzo once. I needed to know more about what had happened. The time had come to drop the restraints of delicacy and ask Mirella directly about it.

By now, Mirella and I were behaving like any two people in love. Except that it was love as it is known by men and women past the first flush of youth; not the joyous, unstinted, romantic attachment of the very young, but a fixation that is to be dealt with warily by both parties.

Our sessions of lovemaking were frequent; a little more frequent, in fact, than our long conversations. It may only have been because she was coming off a stretch of self-enforced celibacy, the chastity of her mourning period, but Mirella seemed to have an animal hunger for sex. She claimed she needed it every day.

It so happened I was seeing her almost daily. But, lightly, I asked, "What would happen if I didn't come around for a couple of days?"

With a shrug, she replied, "Then it's my finger."

There was a coarseness to the answer that put me off a little; it was hardly a line I would have given her counterpart in my novel. Also, it made me wonder if she was seeing me merely as an alternative to her finger, a somewhat superior appendage.

But at least there was a healthy lustiness to our erotic bouts. It wasn't as weird and disturbing as our first time together. I thought back to that night still, and remembered the image I had dimly perceived in the few moments I had come awake—the two shadowy figures in the doorway, Mirella and the mysterious other woman. But now I wasn't sure I hadn't dreamt it, after all.

I had gotten drunk somehow, and the fleeting visions of inebriated half sleep weren't to be trusted. I was someone who fed on his fancies professionally, and Mirella had awakened my imagination, supercharged it. I knew I was capable of hallucinating a spooky climax to the night, just as in childhood, waking from sleep, I had seen ghosts lurking behind the curtain and ominous figures sitting in the chair.

Still, it was as likely as not that the woman who had watched me silently from the doorway was real. In which case, who could she have been? The quiet conversation I had heard—assuming I hadn't imagined it—had been in Italian. What Italian woman could have been wandering around Mirella's house in the early morning hours? I could think of only one possibility—and it was a bizarre one.

The woman might have been Mirella's mother. The Contessa.

I knew that she had escaped from the mental institution and that the authorities had no idea where she was. It was logical to assume that she had fled Italy. And, if she had done so, it was very possible that she had come to this country to try to make contact with her daughter.

Could the Contessa now be living in the house with Mirella? Was that the reason that the seemingly abandoned top floor was kept forever dark, with the curtains always drawn over the windows? Was it the hiding place of the fugitive murderess?

If so, it was a good story. And it was that aspect of it that led me to doubt the whole thing. It was precisely the kind of melodramatic turn of events that I, half-conscious and addled with wine and erotic fever, might have conjured up out of nothing.

I could only speculate on it, since I had no opportunity to check out the matter further. I was never left alone in the house, so I wasn't free to explore on my own, was given no chance to steal up the stairs to find out what or who might be concealed in the darkness at the top.

Mirella, it seemed to me, was being particularly careful about it. I had expected I might stay the night again. But now, after we made love—in that same bedroom, that same bed; I was never invited into the master bedroom—Mirella would put on her robe and wait until I was dressed. Then she would see me to the door.

When we were away from the house, however, things were less constrained. Then we were like any dating couple, moving impulsively about the city in search of diversion. We went to movies, parties, night spots, concerts, art galleries. It was on one of these excursions, on a bright Saturday afternoon after we had been to the Metropolitan Museum, that I brought up the subject of Tobias Walling's death.

At the museum, Mirella hadn't been interested in the classical European paintings—she hadn't needed to come to New York to see Tintorettos, she said—but had wanted to see the primitive art, instead. So we had spent an hour in the new Michael Rockefeller wing, while Mirella, with a bemused smile, had taken in the scary, wood-carved faces of sorcerers and had studied tall poles decorated with evil-looking gnomes with huge phalluses.

Afterward, we entered Central Park and walked down the path to the pond near Seventy-second Street. It was one of the first really warm days of spring, and the area around the pond was well populated. The model-sailboat hobbyists were out in number, their miniature craft skimming over the surface of the pond, describing long, graceful curves in every direction. We found a bench where we could sit and watch the activity on the pond, the sail boats and the splashing dogs, while we talked.

Mirella was telling me about the house she had just bought in Connecticut. It was a made-over farmhouse near Washington Depot in Litchfield County, and the purchase represented, I supposed, her first extravagant use of her new fortune. She was excited by the prospect of being in the country. As soon as she had the house fixed up, she told me, I would come up for the weekend, and we would christen the place together.

At length, when she had exhausted the subject, she fell silent. It was time, I decided, to start asking my questions, the questions I had thought out in advance.

"Mirella," I said, "I've been wondering about something."

"What?"

"Why don't we ever make love in your bed?"

She seemed startled by the question—understandably, since it had come out of nowhere. But I had my reason for asking it, and it had nothing to do with the point I had raised. I thought I knew the answer to the question, anyway.

When she didn't reply immediately, I supplied it. "Is it because it was Tobias's bed?"

"Yes."

"And you feel you would be betraying him if you let another man into it?"

"No, I wouldn't think of it as betrayal," Mirella said. "But there is your bed—and there is Toby's bed." She spoke slowly, carefully, as if she were trying to get hold of a difficult concept. "In a way, he has never left it."

"You still think of him?"

She smiled sadly. "How could I forget him?"

We were silent again. But I had set it up now and was ready to ease into the delicate subject matter I had avoided until then.

"It must have been shattering for you," I said. "I mean, it was so sudden. There were no signs at all, were there? No signs that it was about to happen?"

"Oh, there were signs," she said. "Signs we should have understood—but didn't. We were having too good a time."

"What kind of signs? Pains? Dizziness?"

"Perhaps. I don't know. Toby was not the kind of man who complains. But, that last day, he said his stomach was bothering him. We thought it was the rich food. And all the running around, too— we thought it might have unsettled him."

"You did a lot of socializing?"

"No. Very little, actually. But Toby was so curious, he had to see everything. We went everywhere, to the Cathedral, the Este Castle. And the Etruscan burial place—" she paused uncertainly. "What is the word?"

"Cemetery?"

"More than a cemetery." She thought for a moment. "Necropolis. The necropolis at Spina. They're still digging it up, and it fascinated Toby. We went back there several times. He made friends with one of the archeologists, and they had long talks."

91

This was interesting enough, but I wanted to get back to Walling's symptoms. "And that last day—he had an upset stomach?"

"Yes," she said. "And a pain in his left arm. He mentioned it when we were driving back from Venice."

"You were in Venice?"

"We went there for the day to see Piers Allison. He was passing through. Piers is *always* passing through," she added, with a slight smile. "He was staying at a *pensione* off the Grand Canal."

Mirella was talking about this man as if I should know him, which I didn't. "Who's Piers Allison?" I asked.

"A crazy Englishman. He's very dear to me. You'll meet him," she went on. "He has just written to me. He'll be in New York soon."

Once again we had gotten sidetracked, and I had to bring the conversation back to the point. "Okay," I said, "so you went to Venice to see Piers Allison, and, on the way back, Tobias complained about a pain in his left arm."

"It must have been a severe pain. He asked me to take over the driving. When we got home, Toby seemed to feel a little better. But he was very quiet at dinner. He said he was tired, he wanted to go to bed early. We had a last glass of wine together, then he went to his room."

"He had his own room?"

"Of course, We weren't married yet. Ferrara is not like New York. There were proprieties we had to observe. We didn't want to distress the servants."

"How many servants were there?"

"Only two. Francesca and Gabriele."

"And what was Toby's room like?"

Mirella looked at me, a bit taken aback by the question. "Why do you want to know? It was like any room you sleep in."

"Yes, of course, I realize that." I was being so nakedly eager for the details that I was embarrassing myself. Still, I couldn't let up until I had found out something more. So I persisted. "But, I mean, where was the room? On an upper floor?"

"No," she replied, "it was on the first floor. Just past the *cortile.*"

I was secretly pleased. I had placed Raymond's room in exactly the right place, on the ground floor beyond the courtyard. If my intuition had been correct on this point, perhaps I could trust it on the other guesswork points, too.

"After he went to his room," I asked, "you didn't see him again?"

"Not alive." Mirella, looking away now, seemed to fix her gaze on the feet of the people sauntering by, though I was sure she was seeing nothing at the moment other than the images in her memory. "I should have had some premonition," she said softly. "I was so close to him, I should have known. But he kissed me good night, said, 'See you in the morning,' and I believed it. I believed I *would* see him in the morning. Alive. Happy and laughing, as Toby always was at the beginning of a day."

A Puerto Rican youth walked by, holding a huge transistor radio that was blasting out disco music. But Mirella showed no awarness of the distraction; her expression didn't alter. It was set in a mask of anguish, as she relived a tragedy that had happened in stillness, in a distant part of the world.

"The next morning," she went on, "Francesca woke me. *'Signor Walling è malato,'* she said. But I knew, by the look on here face, that Toby was more than just sick. That something terrible had happened."

Mirella's face convulsed for an instant, as if she was on the verge of tears. It occurred to me that I had never seen her cry.

"I rushed to Toby's room. And I saw him. He was uncovered, and his head was hanging over the side of the bed. There was white foam on his lips and his eyes were open—staring." Her voice faltered and sank to a whisper. "He was dead."

Two large tears emerged from the corners of her eyes and moved slowly down her cheeks. They were not of the moment but were like the tears of a sorrowing statue, as enduring as the very substance of her.

I sat back and looked away. I felt guilty now that I had led her so far back into her pain.

And I was angry, too; angry at all those people who had suspected her, who had maliciously cast doubt on the genuineness of her grief, her innocence.

12

The letter shouldn't have surprised me. My ex-wife had made it clear she was ready to play hardball with me. Still, when I read it, I felt a sudden, sharp nausea, as if I had been punched in the solar plexus. It couldn't have come at a worse time, either psychologically, since I was totally absorbed in my novel, or—more to the point—financially.

Nadine's lawyer established the tenor of his letter in his first lines. Since I had fallen so far behind in my payments, he informed me, his client and he had regretfully decided that it was necessary to take me to court. A suit against me was being initiated. However, the lawyer pointed out, I could still settle the matter by paying the full amount due. He then itemized it for me, the back alimony and the child support—the latter figure greatly swollen by Jeffrey's horrendous orthodontist's bill. The sum total came to a few dollars more than all I had, at the moment, in my bank accounts and my wallet.

I threw down the letter, checked my address book for the number of Nadine's place of employment, a real estate agency in Norwalk, and dialed it then and there.

It was a fairly large firm, and a receptionist answered with the company name. "Is Nadine there?" I asked her.

"Mrs. Hopkins?"

"Yes."

In my mood of the moment, this too irritated me, that Nadine continued to use my name. As far as I was concerned, "Mrs. Hopkins" was my mother, not this woman who was bent on destroying me.

Nadine came onto the line. "Hello?"

"Why are you doing this to me?" I asked.

"You're doing it to yourself, Carl."

She said it in the calm, blissed-out tone of the analysand, a tone of superior enlightenment. The psychoanalysis was something new in her life. I guessed that it was a major reason she still needed my money.

"By your unwillingness to face responsibility," she went on.

"Don't give me that bullshit!"

There was a silence, then Nadine said coolly, "I don't see why you feel it's necessary to call me."

"Because I don't have a lawyer, that's why," I said. "Unlike you, I can't afford one."

"That's your problem," she said.

Had I ever loved this woman? I wondered. The historic fact of it now seemed an incomprehensible aberration.

"Look, Nadine," I said, "don't you see how unreasonable you're being? What do you hope to accomplish by taking me to court?"

"It will make you live up to our agreement."

"You won't get the money. I don't have it."

"We'll let the judge decide that."

"There's nothing to decide. I don't have it."

"Didn't your book just sell to the movies?"

"Where did you hear that?" I asked, in astonishment.

"I heard it somewhere," she said vaguely.

"Well, it's totally false. My agent has been shopping it around. But so far he's come up with nothing."

"Get another agent."

I chose to ignore this. That had been one of her favorite themes while we were married—"Get another agent." Now it didn't seem very pertinent to our discussion.

"Nadine," I said, shifting to a mild, reasonable tone, "if you'll just be patient, I promise I'll pay you everything I owe you."

"What am I supposed to wait for?"

"I'm working on a book right now. I haven't shown it to anyone yet. But I think it could be the big one."

In the ensuing silence, I felt the full force of her skepticism, beamed over the wire to me from Connecticut. Or perhaps I was sensing it from the memory of all those times in the past I had told her that a novel I had just started was going to make the difference.

"An agreement is an agreement," she said, and hung up.

As I usually did when the sordid problems of life became too pressing for me, I plunged still deeper into my work. I could now lose myself in a totally different place, not simply the world of my imagination, but the long-ago world I was researching.

I was reading everything I could find about Ferrara. There'd been very little written about the present-day city, but the chronicled past of the place was rich and vivid. I learned about the great House of Este that ruled Ferrara for centuries. The lords of this family presided over the most brilliant and corrupt court of Renaissance Europe. The Dukes of Ferrara patronized great painters and even greater poets—Ariosto and Tasso—and, at the same time, never hesitated to murder when their anger was roused or their power threatened. The story of Ferrara was of one bloody incident after another: the adulterous wife of an Este ruler beheaded, along with her stepson lover; the unfortunate lover of an Este princess garroted at a banquet table; rival lords hacked to death on country paths or poisoned in distant cities.

At the crest of Ferrara's glory, there appeared the most darkly mysterious figure of all, Lucrezia Borgia. When she arrived in the city to become the Duchess of Ferrara, she was reputed to be the most evil woman in Italy. The bastard daughter of the Pope, she had, by the age of twenty-one, already been through several husbands, one of them murdered by her bloodthirsty brother, Cesare. A substantial body of sinister gossip had built up around her: rumors of incest with her father and her brother, whispers of orgies in the company of Roman courtesans in the papal palace.

And yet, from the time she arrived in Ferrara until her death in the bosom of the Churh, she supposedly lived a blameless life. The sycophantic poets of the court extolled her goodness and charity. No further taint of scandal attached to her name.

Except on one occasion. A handsome young poet, Lucrezia's special favorite, was so rash as to marry the girl he truly loved. Thirteen days after the wedding, he was found dead, with twenty-two stab wounds in his body. The murder was never solved. It remained one of the mysteries of Ferrara.

And Lucrezia Borgia, in the eyes of the historians, remained an enigma. Was she a good-hearted innocent who had been slandered unjustly by the enemies of her family? Or was she a monster who had dissembled, when it was expedient to do so, and concealed her vicious nature? None of the authorities really seemed sure.

I hoped to capture some of this same mystery, this same elusiveness, in the central character of my novel, Isabella Adelardi. In a way I was seeing her as a fictional descendant of Lucrezia Borgia. On the surface she was sweet, joyful, loving. But Raymond, the protagonist, sensed hidden areas in her, dark recesses that might conceal inner demons.

In the course of the story, the atmosphere of danger would intensify around him; he would become aware of a malevolent force threatening him. But he would be uncertain as to the source of the menace. He would suspect and fear that the heart of the evil lay in his beloved Isabella herself.

But he would remain in the palazzo, trapped by his fascination with the woman, fixed by the irresistible attraction of what she embodied, the somber, hypnotic beauty of a dead world.

Like Tobias Walling. Like myself.

Walling had been a romantic and, as Alex Satin had said, enough of a snob to be enticed by an ancient title. He had been in love with exotic lost cultures; the lingering, sepulchral perfume of them had intoxicated him.

I, too, was coming under the same kind of spell. I was beginning to envision myself in another style, as one born in another time. I felt I would have been more properly myself, more true to my innate spirit, in a cape and feathered cap, with a sword hanging at my side— a gentleman-poet, an elegant courtier.

This fantasy was nothing new, of course. As a bookish boy in an Oregon city, born to nothing more than one of the two best hardware stores in town, I had lost myself in the novels of Alexandre Dumas. Victor Hugo and Sir Walter Scott, too, but Dumas had been my favorite. I had sallied forth with D'Artagnan and the Three Musketeers, served with the brave, aristocratic gentlemen of The Forty-Five, wept when my dearest friends had died in duels of honor. I wasn't, then, as the luck of the draw had worked out for me, a drab child of the twentieth century, a stolid descendant of lumberjacks and farmers. I was noble, through and through.

I had not lost these escapist yearnings. I still needed another level of existence, where vengeful ex-wives could not hound me, where money was vulgar and never discussed, where exquisite poetic sentiment was all.

Thus, my affair with Mirella, as I recognized, was part fantasy. Not contemporary at all, it was period romance. If I was fantasizing Mirella as a reincarnation of Lucrezia Borgia, I saw myself as her courtly poet-lover.

I wasn't disturbed by the thought of the historic poet lover, the one who had ended up with twenty-two stab wounds in him. After my conversation with her by the pond, I saw Mirella much the way some scholars saw the "good" Lucrezia—a decent, lovely woman, innocent of any real crime, maligned by petty, envious gossips.

I felt a little guilty about the heavy-handed and insensitive way in which I had questioned her. There was nothing I needed to know about Tobias's death that justified reducing Mirella to tears. And so, the next time I saw her, I avoided any mention of her past tragedies, deciding that, from then on, I would be more delicate about those matters.

However, for my book, I still thought it would be helpful to know some harmless descriptive details. The look of the Ludovisi palazzo, for instance. It seemed likely she had photographs. If so, I was eager to see them.

I had come by her house late in the evening, and we were sitting in the living room, chatting aimlessly for a while as a prelude to going up to bed. Eventually, as she almost always did, Mirella made a reference to her girlhood in Ferrara; this time, she spoke of a pet dog she had particularly loved.

When she concluded her little reminiscence, I said, "You know, darling, there's something you've never done. You've never shown me pictures of your house in Italy. Do you have any?"

"Pictures? Yes, I have some."

"May I see them?"

She nodded, politely acceding to an unremarkable request. We rose and went into the library-den. Mirella took out a picture album from a cabinet, sat beside me on a leather couch, and opened the album in her lap. I looked down over her shoulder at the first photograph.

It was in color, showing the facade of the palazzo. The building was of an impressive size, its massive doorway framed by marble pillars. But I was surprised to see that the facade was quite decayed; it gave the palazzo a run-down, almost slummy appearance. The stucco was very discolored; parts of it had flaked away, revealing the brick behind it.

When, as tactfully as I could, I commented on this, Mirella said, "There is nothing to be done about it. There is much industry around Ferrara. The air is poisoned. It eats away at everything."

I erased this from my mind—industrial blight had no place in my novel—and looked hard at the next photographs in the album. Mirella flipped through them slowly, giving me a few seconds apiece to study them.

There were several of interiors; unlike the facade, they were sumptuous, glowing, and well kept. Most of the furniture, while not modern, was of a much later date than the Cinquecento. But there was one shot of a painted ceiling that was clearly from that earlier period. The subject of the painting was one of the favorite Renaissance fantasies of classical antiquity: youths at play. Semi-naked young men were in motion all over the ceiling, chariot racing, throwing a ball, wrestling.

Then there was a photograph of the courtyard. Rosebushes were in bloom, just as I had imagined. A graceful loggia ran along one end.

The next picture was of Mirella, standing in the courtyard with a boy of her own age. They looked no more than seventeen and they were both smiling brightly.

"Who's the boy?" I asked.

"A friend," she said.

She needed to say nothing more. It was evident that the girl in the picture would have had dozens of young admirers. I had thought that the Mirella I knew was at the peak of her beauty. But, looking at this photograph, I saw that I was wrong. Mirella had actually faded somewhat. She seemed a mere human now, not the breathtaking goddess in the picture who was as perfect as any of the painted creatures on the palace ceilings.

She flipped to the next photograph. It was of a man in a dark suit, standing by a fireplace. His jacket was buttoned and the three points of the handkerchief were impeccable in his breast pocket. The photograph had a formal look to it, as if it had been taken for some special occasion.

"Your father?" I asked.

Mirella nodded.

I took the album from her to look at the photograph more closely. Count Ludovisi was a lean, silver-haired, handsome man; rather severe-looking in this shot, but it might have been because he had felt uncomfortable in front of a camera.

I went on to the next photograph. It was a more casual shot of the count and another, younger man. They were sitting in a book-lined study, and they were both tweedy, tieliess, and smiling.

I had little doubt of who the other man was. Still, I asked, "Gianfranco?"

"Yes."

There was something about this photograph that was disturbing me. I couldn't figure out what it was.

With Mirella watching me, I didn't want to continue staring at the photograph, so I went on to what followed it in the album.

There were two empty plastic holders, and then two more photographs that concluded the picture series: Mirella again, in the company of girlfirneds.

I paid little attention to them. I was thinking about those two empty plastic holders. I was sure that they had once held photographs of someone.

And it was obvious who the missing person was in this family album, the person who would have logically followed Count Ludovisi in the sequence. Mirella's mother, the Contessa.

As I glanced up from the album, I was fixed for a moment by Mirella's intense gaze. I sensed that she was guessing my thought.

Then it struck me, suddenly, what it was that I had been on the verge of recognizing in the photograph of her father and her mother's lover. I turned back to it quickly and studied Gianfranco's features— the short nose with the broad nostrils, the thin mouth.

Gianfranco and I resembled each other rather strikingly.

Mirella took the album from me. "Enough of the past," she said and closed it.

13

He was a man who suggested thorns and weeds. Sunburned and stringy, with dry, unruly hair, a scraggly red beard, and toughened hands that bore the marks of healing scratches, he seemed distinctly out of place in Mirella's living room. In his dirty safari jacket and discolored corduroy trousers, he looked as if he had just emerged from tangled underbrush.

Meeting him came as a surprise. When I arrived at the house to take Mirella out to dinner, I expected that, as always, she would be waiting for me alone. But Porfiria greeted me at the door, rather than her mistress, which meant that Mirella was otherwise occupied. When I entered the living room, I saw that she had company. This odd, travel-worn man was sitting across from her in the armchair.

Mirella and the man rose simultaneously and turned to me. "Carl," Mirella said, "I want you to meet a dear friend of mine, Piers Allison."

I remembered the name. He was the person that she and Tobias Walling had visited in Venice, that last day of Walling's life.

"It's a pleasure to meet you, Piers," I said.

"You're the novelist?" he asked, as he shook my hand.

"You know my work?"

"No," Piers said. "But Mirella was just telling me about you."

I may have seemed a bit crestfallen, because he hastened to add, "I'm sure I should know your work. It doesn't mean anything that I don't." With a laugh, he said, "Where I've been, the only things to read are the backs of medicine bottles."

His English accent, I noticed, was upper-class. His exterior may have been scruffy, but he clearly hadn't been born to be a luckless vagabond. Rather, I suspected, he was a renegade from the pampered, privileged life.

"Where have you been?" I asked

"Mexico."

"The Yucatan?"

"Right on the button!" he exclaimed brightly, as if he was astonished at my keen intuition.

"Well, you don't seem the city type," I said.

"Oh, I've spent my time in cities, old chum. Lived *here* for a while, as a matter of fact. That's when I first met Mirella." He glanced at her inquiringly. "How long ago was that?"

"Ten or eleven years," she replied.

"She was a baby," Piers said gallantly.

"But you've seen each other in Italy, too," I said.

Piers seemed momentarily perplexed by this comment. Then, casually, he said, "Yes. Yes, we have. When our paths have crossed."

Mirella's face had clouded. But then, with sudden brightness, she changed the subject. "Piers had just arrived here. He came in on the morning plane."

"Yes. Pardon my appearance," Piers said to me, without real apology. "This is practically all I have to wear. I left my wardrobe at the bottom of a river near Campeche. Our boat overturned."

"Rough water?" I asked.

"Unfriendly locals."

He obviously had a story to tell, but this didn't seem to be the time to solicit it. So I asked politely, "Where are you staying here?"

"At the YMCA."

"Oh? YOU want the use of a gym?"

"I hardly need exercise, old chum," he said, with a short laugh. "It's the best I can afford—" he paused to give Mirella a quick look and what might have been a meaningful smile"—at the present low ebb in my fortunes."

This led to a moment of silence, with Piers still smiling and Mirella expressionless. Then, rather abruptly, she spoke up. "Piers just came by for a few minutes. He knows we're going out to dinner. I'll get ready." As she started out, she said, over her shoulder, "Fix yourself a drink, Carl, if you want."

This last suggestion seemed a good one. I took a step in the direction of the bar, but then paused to ask Piers, "Anything for you?"

He held up the glass he was holding. "I'm content with this Perrier, thanks."

I went through the archway to the dining room, poured myself a scotch-on-the-rocks at the bar, and then returned to the living room and sat opposite Piers. We regarded each other pleasantly for a moment.

At length I asked, "Are you an explorer or a prospector?"

"A little bit of both," he said. "But I'm not precisely either. Actually, I'm a scientist." With a wry smile, he added, "Though you might find people who'd argue *that*, too."

"Why? Are you into something disreputable?"

"Oh, definitely. In the eyes of the scientific establishment, anything that goes against its approved procedures is disreputable. If you don't hide away in some bloody million-dollar laboratory, but, instead, go out among primitive peoples to find their secrets, you're not only a crank, you're a scoundrel, a traitor to the scientific method." He indicated his soiled outfit with a gesture and said, "As you see, I'm not a recipient of foundation grants."

"What are you? A biologist?"

"By training, I'm a chemist," he replied. "I took my degree in organic chemistry at Cambridge—with honors. I was a promising youth." He laughed. "I didn't go bad until later."

"And what are the secrets you find among primitive peoples?"

"I try to find what hasn't been found already—which isn't easy. My line of research goes back a long way, you know. The Chinese were at it thousands of years ago, and the East Indians and the Arabs after them. The properties of mandrake and belladonna, for instance, have been known from the earliest times. So I have to go to the remotest places—some of them pretty hairy—to find anything new."

"You concentrate on herbs?"

"Vegetable drugs, yes. Animal drugs, too. Whatever is being used. I find it, test it for its properties, then chemically analyze it."

"Is this anthropology? Or is it relevant to modern medical science?"

"Well, it isn't just quaint folklore, if that's what you mean." The touch of annoyance in his tone had a weariness to it, as if he had had to argue this point too many times. "Where do you think our drugs came from in the first place? You can find a whole medicine cabinet growing out of the ground. Digitalis came from foxglove, morphine from the white poppy, castor oil for the castor bean, and scopolamine—the truth serum—can be found in any number of herbs, like jimson weed and black henbane."

"What were you researching in Mexico?" I asked. "Peyote?"

"I'm afraid mescaline is old hat by now," Piers said. "A thousand hippie chemists have beaten me to it. But the hallucinogen I *have* done quite a lot of work on is muscarine."

"What's that?"

"It's derived from the fly agaric mushroom."

"The magic mushroom?"

"It's been called that. It's used in primitive religions all over the world. I've sampled it myself. It gives you visions beyond anything you could try." With a shrug, he added, "If you need visions."

"Doesn't everyone?"

"I rather imagine so."

"You were looking for magic mushrooms down in the Yucatan?"

"This trip? No, I was studying toads."

"Toads?"

"The Bufo. It's a giant tropical toad. You can find Bufos from the Yucatan down through Brazil. The Indians of western Columbia use the poison from Bufo skins on their arrow tips."

"You're interested in poisons, too?"

"Not as such," he said. "But one man's poison can be another man's miracle drug. A Bufo compound does wonders for sinus conditions."

This flow of arcane information, I realized, could go on indefinitely. He was spilling over with it, and it didn't seem to matter to him whether or not he had a listener who was really interested. As it happened, I found much of it fascinating. But what I was curious about was Piers Allison's personal story, not his professional specialty.

"How did you happen to get into this field?" I asked. "I mean, why did you break away from the establishment?"

"I was led astray by a rich American wife," Piers replied. "A Texas lady. She only felt comfortable in backward nations. So we settled in Morocco—in Fez—where she dabbled in mysticism and I, lacking anything else to do, browsed around in medieval Arab science."

"What happened to your wife, finally?"

"She became caught up in Scientology, and she ran off—to do whatever it is very rich Scientologists do. I was left to myself." With a light gesture, he concluded, "And so my travels began."

Mirella returned, wearing her coat. She had caught Piers's last words as she came in, and she said to him now, "You'll have to tell him the rest of your life story some other time, Piers. Carl and I have to get to the restaurant before we lose our reservations."

I had told her nothing about a reservation; there wasn't any. It was clear that she didn't want us to linger with Piers any longer. I put down my glass and rose.

Piers rose also. "It's quite all right," he said. "I was about to go."

"I enjoyed meeting you, Piers," I said. "I hope we have a chance to talk further."

This was something more than polite interest on my part. I wanted to hear what he had to say about certain subjects we had left unmentioned.

Tobias Walling, in particular, and that last afternoon the three of them had spent together in Venice.

"Are you going to stay in New York for a while?" I asked.

"I'll be around," Piers said, with a smile.

14

In early May, Mirella gave a dinner party. It wasn't a large, ambitious affair, but, rather, a simple dinner for eight—which may have been the largest number she felt she could handle in her first venture as a hostess at the East Eighty-fourth Street house. More than that and the gathering might slip out of her control. As I discovered that evening, Mirella was feeling too insecure in her new role as mistress of this house—Tobias Walling's house—to risk that.

Eve Lukas, as might have been expected, was there. I knew that Eve had developed ambiguous feelings toward Mirella. But still the historic fact remained: she was Mirella's oldest friend in New York. Piers Allison, with a haircut, a trimmed beard, and looking quite respectable in an expensive new suit, was, more or less, paired off with Eve.

Janice, Alex Satin's great love, was there also, with her Swede, a chunky, middle-aged blond who may or may not have been named Lars—I only heard the name once. I hadn't been aware that Mirella knew Janice particularly well. I guessed that their acquaintance was, in actuality, fairly slight and that Janice was simply serving the same function here that she had at so many other dinner parties, that of the "lovely, quiet girl," the bland, ornamental young woman who would enhance the visual effect but ruffle the atmosphere no more than the vase of roses on the side table.

This could have been said as well of the fourth man present, whom I, along with the other guests, was meeting for the first time—a youngish, handsome fellow named Larry Booth. If he hadn't had an authentic look of wealth to him, I would have pegged him as a male model. He was the Ivy League male ideal, regular of feature and perfect down to his wrinkle-free socks. But he had the gloss and lack of weight of a slick magazine page; it was as if the surface of him was the whole of what there was to get. He smiled a lot and said all the right things, none of which I could remember ten seconds after they were spoken. During the introductions, Mirella had explained to the rest of us that Larry was her new neighbor in Connecticut.

And then there was the surprise guest—a surprise to me, anyway. Sasha Rombeck. The last person to arrive, she had been subdued and clearly uneasy from the moment she had joined us. This was, I was sure, the first time Sasha had set foot in her ex-lover's house since his death.

I couldn't imagine why Mirella had invited her, or, for that matter, why Sasha had come. But I had to wait to satisfy my curiosity about it. As we sat around the living room, sipping our drinks and savoring the hors d'oeuvres, we conversed as a group. Mirella kept the small talk moving around the circle, addressing each of us in turn with exquisite courtesy, or perhaps from a reluctance to let any private conversation start up independently.

Finally, though, she had to retire to the kitchen to consult with Porfiria about the dinner, and then we did, indeed, fragment into twos and threes. I changed my seat and sat beside Sasha, who, up until that point, had said almost nothing.

"Have you made up with Mirella?" I asked her.

Sasha looked at me intently, almost suspiciously. "Why do you ask?"

"Because you're here."

"I'm here because she invited me." She paused. "I don't dare *not* be here."

There was a grimness in Sasha's tone, and a suggestion of fear that made me wonder. I remembered her distraught state when I had run into her on Washington Square, but I had thought that that particular torment was in the past. I had assumed that Mirella, since then, had abandoned her cruel telephone game with Sasha, the sudden nocturnal calls, the mocking recitation over the wire of the damning entries in Walling's journal. But now I wasn't so sure.

"It's still going on?" I asked.

"Don't you know?" An edge of bitterness came into her voice. "You should know all about it. You're so cozy with her."

"No, I don't know," I said. "That's the truth."

After a moment she said quietly, "It's still going on. Worse than ever."

Larry Booth joined us. His smile was bright and his tight, golden curls seemed to glow with his eagerness to please.

"I understand you work with old buildings," he said to Sasha. It was a direct, friendly conversation-opener. Also, it revealed that he had been informed in advance about her job with the Landmarks Preservation Commission.

"That's right," she replied.

"I have an interest in them myself," Larry said.

"You're an architect?" she asked.

"No." Off-handedly, and with a touch of complacence, he said, "I buy them sometimes."

I felt I had nothing to contribute to this conversation, so I went over to talk with Piers Allison. He had just returned from a visit to the bar, where he had refilled his glass to the brim with Perrier water, generously iced. It was as if the thirst he had brought back with him from the jungle had yet to be quenched.

"You're looking good, Piers," I said.

"You're looking good, too, old chum," he replied genially.

He had interpreted it as the usual pleasantry, but, in fact, I had meant it in the more specific sense. "Thanks," I said. "But you're looking particularly spiffy. I hardly recognized you." With a gesture, I indicated his lustrous three-piece suit. "This didn't end up at the bottom of the Campeche?"

"It was on the rack at Brooks Brothers until a few days ago," he said. "This is my first time out in these duds."

"Well, it gives you a different image, that's for sure. Are you still at the Y?"

"No, I've moved from there. I'm staying at the Volney now."

This, I knew, was a chic residential hotel on the Upper East Side. It was far from inexpensive.

"You seem to be doing well. Did a foundation come through for you?" I asked lightly.

He laughed. "The Mirella Foundation."

"She's helped you out, huh?"

"She's been a good friend to me."

And a generous one, I thought. She obviously had given him something more than a mere handout.

"Well, she has the money now," I commented. "What else is money for but to help friends?"

"What else, indeed?" he agreed. Then he added, "I'm sure old Toby wouldn't have begrudged it me."

It was the first time I had heard him refer to Tobias Walling. I paused, wondering if I should follow up on this little opening. But then I let it pass.

"Mirella is a great lady," I said.

"A great and a good lady," Piers said.

I looked at him uncertainly. Had his reverential tone been that genuine? Or had I detected a sardonic note in it?

Mirella returned and announced that dinner was served. We all went into the dining room, admired the splendor of the table arrangement—Mirella had put out the best of the Ludovisi china, crystal, and silver—searched out our place cards, and sat. Mirella had positioned me at the opposite end of the table from her. Sasha was on my right and Piers on my left. Mirella, at the head of the table, had Larry and Janice on either side of her. Eve and the Swede faced each other across the middle of the table.

The conversation was tentative at the outset. But then the Swede happened to comment on the clams on the half shell that were being served as the opening course. He said that he had been a little fearful of shellfish ever since he had contracted hepatitis. It was a graceless statement in the circumstances, but it was enough to give Piers a cue for one of his colorful disquisitions.

"I think there *should* be some element of danger in eating another animal," Piers offered. "Some of the greatest delicacies you taste at the risk of your own life. Have any of you ever had fugo stew?"

He looked around the table, as if he actually expected an affirmative answer. Then Eve, speaking for all of us, said, "I don't even know what it is."

"It's made from the puffer fish," Piers said. "It's one of the most prized dishes in Japan. The puffer is absolutely delicious—but it does present a problem. Every organ of it contains fugo poison, a poison so deadly that the tiniest bit of it, just eight or ten milligrams, can kill you."

"Then how can they eat it?" Larry asked. "I mean, how do they get the poison out?"

"With extreme care," Piers replied. "Japanese cooks have to go to a special school and get a diploma before they're allowed to cook fugo. They learn a complicated technique to extract the poison. Even so, there are accidents. Fugo aficionados kick off at the rate of a hundred every year."

"That's awful!" Janice said, with a fetching look of horror. "I don't think I'd want to try it."

"But wouldn't you find it exciting, dear lady?" Piers asked. "Savoring a one-in-ten-thousand chance of death on your taste buds?" He laughed. "I imagine that's a big part of the dish's appeal."

"This is fascinating, Piers," Mirella said, smiling sweetly. "But do we really have to talk about it? Our main course is fish."

Just at that moment, Porfiria appeared with the main course, which was, indeed, sea bass prepared in a wine sauce. We turned our attention to it, helping ourselves from the serving plate as it came around. The conversation shifted to topics more compatible with the pleasure of eating.

The dinner progressed smoothly. Mirella presided over it with an assurance and ease that reminded me that she had been raised to do precisely this—sit at the head of an elegant table while favored guests were fed beautifully. She made sure that the conversation never faltered and, at the same time, kept an eye on the details of the service. Every so often, she would murmur a quiet command in Spanish to Porfiria and the servant would respond to it promptly and efficiently. The various dishes and wines came and went with the exact timing of a military operation. Through it all, Mirella sat with her head held high, her posture gracefully erect, her cheeks flushed with a mild elation, as if she were an accomplished horsewoman who, after a long layoff, had found herself in the saddle again.

At length, Larry raised his wineglass. "I think we should toast our beautiful hostess," he said.

"Hear, hear!" Piers said.

"With thanks for bringing us together," Larry went on, "for this—" He looked at Mirella inquiringly. "It's the first dinner here, isn't it?"

"Yes," Mirella said. "This is my first dinner party in this house."

"And I'm sure there'll be many more such lovely occasions here," Larry said, concluding the toast and drinking.

We all joined in, taking the ritual sip of wine. Even Sasha, who had sat in near silence through the dinner, responding only in monosyllables to the Swede's attempts at conversation, dutifully brought her glass to her lips.

"I would like to propose another toast," Mirella said. "To one who is not here"—her dark eyes filled with sorrow—"who can never be here in life now, but whose spirit, I know, is with us tonight." She raised her glass. "To my beloved Toby."

We drank again. All except Sasha, who stopped her glass halfway and lowered her eyes.

"I had my fears about this dinner," Mirella went on, in a more conversational tone. "Because I knew someone would be here who had been in this house many times before. Who may have sat here, where I am, at other dinners." She looked at Sasha and smiled. "Have I done this properly, Sasha? Have I lived up to—what would you call it?—the tradition?"

There were uneasy faces around the table now. Not everyone there may have known about Sasha's past relationship with Walling, but the malice underlying Mirella's silken tone was perceptible, and it was an uncomfortable moment.

Sasha, however, tried to act as if it were a well-intentioned question. Politely, she answered, "Yes, Mirella, you're doing this beautifully."

"Good," Mirella said. "It means a lot to me—hearing *you* say that." She looked at Larry. "Sasha was very close to Toby. Did you know that, Larry?"

Larry seemed startled at being addressed. "No, I didn't."

"Eve remembers those days," Mirella went on. "Did you ever wonder, Eve, why Toby and Sasha were so close?"

Eve glanced sideways at Sasha. Sasha was staring at Mirella, with the blank helplessness of a fixed prey, and her cheeks were reddening.

"Let's talk about something else," Eve said quietly.

Mirella ignored this. "I understand now," she said. "I understand why Toby meant so much to Sasha." She gazed at Sasha again, and her eyes had a meaningful gleam in them. "He was like a father to her."

There was a silence at the table. I was perhaps the only one, other than Sasha, who understood what Mirella was referring to. But the stunned, pained look on Sasha's face made any attempt to resume the conversation impossible.

"Doesn't that happen with so many of us?" Mirella asked, in a musing tone, as if she were merely waxing philosophical. "Transferring our love for our fathers to other men? The same kind of love?"

With rising horror, I wondered if she were actually going to mention it—the shocking revelation in Walling's journal. It would have been far beyond the pale of decency, but Mirella, calmly in control, luxuriating in her power over her former rival, seemed unconcerned with conventional limits.

"Tell us about your father, Sasha," she said.

"Excuse me," Sasha said, and rose quickly.

She fled from the room. We all sat, unmoving, as we listened to the sound of her receding footsteps, and then the opening and closing of the house door.

The guests didn't stay late. By eleven, Mirella and I were alone again.

Mirella was still filled with energy. She moved around the living room, tidying up, putting ashtrays back in place, all the while talking, reliving the dinner party.

"Larry is a charming man, isn't he?" she said. "And Piers—I hardly recognized him in his new clothes. *All* the men were attractive. That Swede isn't bad-looking—for such a bore. And you, Carl, you were the most handsome of all. You must always wear those gold cufflinks. I love you in cufflinks."

She chattered on brightly, almost elatedly, as if she were talking about a social event that had been an unquestioned triumph. It was as if she had forgotten about the ugly moment that had climaxed the dinner—or, at least, had dismissed it from her mind.

But I hadn't. And I wasn't going to let it pass.

"Why did you do it?" I asked suddenly.

Mirella stopped in the midst of reaching for an emptied candy tray and turned to me. With a puzzled frown, she asked, "Why did I do what?"

"You know what I'm talking about," I said. "That number you did on poor Sasha. What kind of woman are you? How can you be so cruel?"

"I told you, Carl," she said quietly, "I am not a nice person. I do not forgive those who harm me."

"And so you're still punishing her—because you think she's talking against you?"

"It's not just that. She hurt me before, too. The first time I came to this house."

"You saw her here before?"

"Yes. When *she* was sleeping here every night. When *she* was the lady of the house. Toby had just met me and he invited me here to a dinner party. It was a small dinner, like this one, but that night it was Sasha who sat at the head of the table." Mirella's mouth tightened. "She was terrible to me."

"Maybe she already suspected that Toby was interested in you."

"Perhaps. But I don't think so. She was just being an arrogant bitch. I was a nobody to her—a foreigner—a wop woman with no money. And she let me know it."

She had said this with the full force of a bitterness that, by all rights, should have faded away by then. Clearly, it hadn't. And the

114

incident with Sasha, I guessed, wasn't the only memory of its kind. The pain she revealed now seemed too well inhabited. There probably had been other slights, too, real and fancied, in her deprived New York years that lived on in her, in much the same way as unhealed wounds.

"You may have been overly sensitive," I commented.

"How can you know?" she asked, in a hard challenging voice. "Do you know what it's like to be a stranger here, with a name that sounds funny to people, and to be without money and alone? Sasha—she is only three or four generations away from some German thief or draft dodger. But her family has money, so she could play the grand lady with me. Breeding, a respected name, centuries of tradition—these things have no meaning in this country. Money! Money is everything!"

"Well, now you have it," I said.

"Yes," Mirella said, with a bright, triumphant smile, "now I have money. And I will do exactly what I want. Because I can pay for it. That's the American way, no? Now I, too, can be an American!"

15

A couple of days later, Alex Satin phoned me.

There were no pleasantries; he got right to the point. "Okay, tell me about it," he said. "Tell me about the dinner party where you saw Janice."

I was a little startled. "How do you know about that?" I asked.

"From Janice. She told me"

"Well, if she has already described it to you, what can I add?"

"Tell me about Janice," he urged.

I wasn't quite sure what he was after. "She looked gorgeous," I said.

"I'm sure she did," Alex said impatiently. "But who was she with?"

I paused now. "You mean, she didn't tell you?"

"No." His voice grew agitated. "All she would say was that she was with a man. She was very casual about it—but she wouldn't tell me who the man was. She said it was someone I wouldn't know. But somehow I didn't believe her."

"Uh-huh," I replied noncommittally.

"Tell me, Carl! Tell me as a friend. Was it the Swede?"

There seemed to be no point in keeping it from him. "Yes, as a matter of fact, it was."

"I knew it!" he cried out, in a strangled voice. "I knew it!"

Hearing the violence of his reaction, I wondered if I had been imprudent. But then, before I could feel guilty about it, the logical thought occurred to me. "Janice must have expected you to find out," I said. "Otherwise, she wouldn't have told you she was at this party, in the first place."

"Oh, sure," he agreed. "But she wanted to make me work for it. Sweat it out. That's the way she is. Oh, that wretched woman!" he moaned, with a masochist's relish.

"Do you want to know anything else, Alex? Or can I go back to my work?"

"Well—" he paused. "Did she seem to be having a good time?"

"About as good a time as anyone had, considering. Did she tell you what happened?"

"You mean, with Mirella and Sasha?"

"Yes."

"Janice seemed a little confused about it. She told me that Mirella said something to Sasha that drove her out of the house. But she couldn't understand what it was."

"I don't think anyone there could," I said. "The point was *Sasha* could."

"It must have been a corker, whatever it was," Alex said. "Sasha has left town."

"What? How do you know?"

"I called Sasha before I called you. Or tried to, anyway. She wasn't at her office. They said she had gone to the country somewhere. She's taken a leave of absence—for health reasons."

I remembered the stricken look on Sasha's face the moment before she fled the table, and I felt suddenly uneasy. "She seemed all right to me," I said.

"Don't be obtuse," Alex said, his voice turning cold. "Your girlfriend has been playing games with Sasha's head. This last thing must have done the trick."

His wording put it squarely on me: "your girlfriend." It implied that he saw me as a guilty accomplice in Mirella's actions. Perhaps, I realized, my other friends were seeing me in that way, too.

"I had nothing to do with it, Alex," I said.

"I shouldn't think so," he said. "But I've been wondering."

"What do you wonder?"

"Well, Mirella and you have become such a loving twosome. And she's a monster! It's a mystery to me, Carl. What have you found in common with her?"

"I have my reasons for this relationship," I said, after a moment.

"Sex? Is it that much greater with her?"

117

"It's pretty good, actually. But that's not the main reason."

"Then what is?"

I knew it might be unwise to explain further. But at the same time I couldn't bear the idea of letting Alex go on in his misunderstanding of me. I had few enough friends as it was; I couldn't afford to lose his friendship.

"If I told you, Alex, would you swear to keep it secret?"

"Sure."

I doubted that this perfunctory oath gave me much security, but I went ahead, anyway.

"I'm writing a novel," I said.

"So?"

"Mirella is the inspiration for it. It's sort of based on Tobias and her."

"You're writing a novel about *that?*" The shock was perceptible in his voice.

"That's right."

"And this is what you're up to? You're having an affair with Mirella just so you can learn about her?"

"It's oversimplifying it. But you could say that, I guess."

There was a silence.

"That's sick," he said.

I bridled a bit. Alex, with his hang-ups, hardly seemed to be in a position to accuse me, or anyone else, of perverse behavior.

"If I get a good book out of this," I said, "it isn't sick. It's the end result that counts."

"Maybe. If you think end results are what life is about. But you should watch yourself, Carl," he said quietly. "You should watch what you do to yourself on the way to that end result."

The weather was perfect during my first weekend at Mirella's country house. The air had a seductive feel that made it impossible to stay inside—and Mirella's place, a rather Spartan farmhouse that hadn't been improved much beyond its original state, wasn't set up for lounging around in, anyway. So we devoted most of our time to outdoor activities. We swam in the river that ran through the canyon behind her property. We took walks in the woods. And we spent an afternoon playing tennis.

The tennis court belonged to her neighbor, Larry Booth. Larry's house was only a hundred yards down the road, but it was almost the polar opposite of Mirella's place. It was modern and equipped with every imaginable appliance. The tennis court had lights for nighttime playing. The swimming pool had an adjoining sauna. There was a barbecue pit and a gazebo. The property was like an oasis of Scarsdale luxury set down in the midst of rural Connecticut.

Larry was alone that weekend and he seemed eager for our company—or, at least, for a tennis partner. He volleyed gently with Mirella for a while, and then he got down to the serious business of the game with me. I played two sets with him and didn't take a game from him in either set.

I was a little embarrassed; I had wanted to make a creditable showing in front of Mirella. But Larry was a few years younger than I and more of a physical type. I couldn't, however, also rationalize that he took better care of himself. Afterward, as we sprawled in lawn chairs beside the tennis court, he drank down a very dry martini while chain-smoking Dunhill cigarettes to build up his nicotine level again.

Mirella gave most of her attention to Larry. She showed her admiration of the victorious athlete with little touches on his arm and quick, bright smiles. I felt a twinge of jealousy, but had to accept the situation. It was as if we were two knights who had jousted in the lists, and now the winner was being rewarded by our beautiful sovereign's favor.

That night, though, as we got ready for bed, I had her to myself again. There was no mention of tennis or Larry Booth; we had cut off the memory of the afternoon with the closing of the bedroom door. We were by now settled-in lovers, and, while there was the usual unspoken anticipation as we undressed, our talk was of commonplace, domestic matters. We were past the need to impress each other conversationally.

Mirella was telling me her decorating ideas for the still only half-furnished country house. I might have expected her to recreate an Italian villa. Instead, she had fallen in love with all things Early American. She had been prowling the local antique shops, and one of her recent finds was on the bedroom wall, a framed woolen sampler with the unremarkable motto, "God Bless Our Home."

I said little in response. My thoughts were far away from such homey concerns. My mind was focused on my current personal problem, one that was turning into a nightmare for me.

My ex-wife and her attorney had carried out their threat. The machinery of the law had been set in motion against me and I had been summoned to appear in court.

I had been forced to retain my own lawyer, but his counsel had been of little comfort. He had pointed out the dire consequences for me, present and future, if an unfavorable court judgment were handed down. He could offer only one solution, and that a temporary one. We had to arrange an out-of-court settlement. It would inevitably involve a substantial part payment of the money I owed Nadine.

But I lacked the funds for even this stopgap measure. I felt totally helpless to extricate myself from the situation. And my growing sense of desperation was starting to take its toll on my work. In recent days I had sometimes been so overcome with anxiety that I was unable to compose a comprehensible sentence.

I knew that I shouldn't be letting it affect me so drastically. The lack of necessary cash was the most banal of all problems, and it was usually solved, one way or the other. Piers Allison, for instance, after his Yucatan disaster, had found himself broke. And he had been put back on his feet by his friend, Mirella.

Remembering this, a thought had occurred to me—if Mirella had been so generous with a friend, would she not be equally generous with a lover?

I had some hesitations about it. I wasn't normally the type who put the touch on people. Besides, in this case, asking for financial help might inject a sour element into our romance. But then, I reminded myself, Mirella wasn't simply the girl I was sleeping with; she was a New York rich lady. New York rich ladies were a special breed, and they had their obligations, to worthy causes, needy artists, friends and lovers who were in trouble.

"What are you thinking?" Mirella asked suddenly. She had become aware, by now, that I wasn't listening to what she was saying.

"Oh, I'm sorry," I said, apologizing for my inattention. "It's just that I've got something on my mind. Something that's been bugging me lately."

"What is it?"

I told her. I related the whole story of my difficulties with my ex-wife. It was the first time I had really gone into it with her. It was, I knew, a rather grubby situation, one that didn't make me look good, and I had avoided mentioning it in the past.

But now I was frank and complete with her. Mirella listened with polite sympathy; perhaps, even, a touch of enjoyment, since she never seemed to mind hearing other women spoken of poorly—and I wasn't giving Nadine a good report.

When I concluded, though, by specifying my need for a substantial amount of money, her half smile faded and her expression turned cautiously blank. She was getting the point finally, of why I was telling her all this.

"How much do you need?" she asked.

"Two thousand would do it, I think."

"That's a lot of money."

"Yes, I suppose it is."

I felt embarrassed and a little annoyed. I hadn't even asked her for it—not directly, anyway—and yet Mirella, the possessor of millions, seemed to be already balking at the sum involved. As it happened, it wasn't nearly enough, the bare minimum I required.

At length she said, "I think I might be able to help you."

"Oh, would you?" I brightened. "I'd pay it back as soon as I could."

Mirella was regarding me now with a peculiar, contained smile that made me uneasy. Her eyes were fixed on me appraisingly.

"We'll talk about it later," she said. "Let's make love."

She resumed undressing. I was startled by her abruptness, but I, too, finished undressing. When we were both naked, we sat beside each other on the bed. Nothing more had been said, but I knew I had to please her now, please her more than I ever had before. I started to take her into my arms.

"No," she said. "Lie down."

I stretched out on the bed, lying on my side, propping myself on one elbow.

"On your back," she said.

I rolled onto my back and lay still.

"Don't move," she said. "Don't touch me with your hands at all."

I obeyed. And I obeyed each of her commands after that. I kissed the bare foot she held to my lips, kissed it and licked it. When she straddled my face, I stimulated her with my lips and tongue.

I was suffocating and the faintly bitter taste almost made me gag. But I did what she wanted me to do, did it until she climaxed.

I came, too, convulsively, even though I hadn't joined with her. But there was no pleasure in it. I felt soiled, sick with shame.

She separated from me. I lay motionless, my eyes closed. I sensed the lightening of weight on the mattress as she got up.

After a few moments, I opened my eyes again. I saw that Mirella was sitting at a table, with her checkbook before her. She was writing out a check.

She tore out the check, rose, came back to me, and dropped it on the bedside table. "There you are," she said. "Your two thousand dollars."

16

I was making progress on my book. One-third of it was done and I had started the chapter in which Raymond was to get his first glimpse of Isabella's mother, the Marchesa.

Raymond, at this point in the story, was no longer in ignorance of what had happened in the Adelardi family. He had learned the secret his fiancée had long withheld from him—the shocking crime that had cast a permanent shadow on the everyday life at the palazzo.

Isabella's mother had murdered her handsome, faithless lover. She had stabbed him in the heart and left him dying on the marble floor of the main hall of the palazzo, with the painted images of the Adelardi ancestors gazing down at him.

The Marchesa had disappeared immediately after the murder. Raymond had been led to believe that she was a fugitive in some other country.

But, in the section I now wrote, he discovered otherwise:

Raymond reached the top of the stairs and paused, a little breathless from his long climb up. He wondered if he should stop there and go no farther. It would be embarrassing if someone came upon him prowling about the top floor of the palazzo, furtive as a thief.

It was unlikely, though, that anyone would. In the week he had been there, he had seen no one go up these stairs, neither the servants nor Isabella herself. The top floor seemed to have been abandoned as excess space, unneeded now that there was only one last member of the family left in the palazzo.

But then, if no one ever went up there, what was the reason for the mysterious light he had seen from the street, the night before, in a window in the uppermost turret of the palazzo? It hadn't been the bright, functional illumination that would have been used by a servant fetching something or doing a chore. Rather, it had been a dim glow that had barely touched the window, the secretive light that might have been cast by a shielded lamp.

He realized that there was probably some quite ordinary explanation for it. Still, it had stimulated his curiosity about this abandoned top floor. That curiosity had gotten the best of him and now, taking advantage of Isabella's brief absence from the palazzo, he had ascended the five flights of stairs to do a little exploring on his own.

Raymond found himself in a hall that enclosed the landing area. An archway led out to what seemed to be a long, windowed gallery. He turned away from the archway to take in the rest of the hall. The doors around him were closed. It was clear that no maid had been there recently. The side table had a thick layer of dust on it and the chair beside it was covered with a stained white cloth. A large cobweb had formed in one corner of the ceiling.

Suddenly, he sensed that someone was behind him. The back of his neck prickled, as if it were being chilled by a cold, intent gaze. He turned, but not quickly enough to get a look at the woman who had been standing in the archway, watching him. He only caught a glimpse of the fabric of her long, black dress; the swirling hem of it was there at the edge of the archway for an instant, and then was gone.

Raymond hesitated uncertainly for a moment. Then he rushed through the archway and looked down the long, narrow gallery. The woman was some distance from him, hurrying away. From behind, all he could see was that she was a tall woman in black, with her dark hair tightly curled in a bun.

He ran after her. "Wait!" he called out. "Signora, please! Aspetti! Wait!"

When the woman reached the end of the gallery, she stopped, turned, and stared at him. He came to a quick halt, fixed to the spot by her burning gaze.

I sat back and thought over the last sentence. A few paragraphs back, her gaze had "chilled" Raymond. Could it "burn" him now?

Fire and ice—why not? I decided I would let it stand.

124

The time had come to describe the Marchesa. I knew it should be a moment of instant recognition for Raymond. But it occurred to me that I hadn't established that he had seen a picture of her.

Well, that could easily be fixed. I had made references to the portraits that were on the walls throughout the palazzo. I could insert a brief section into an earlier chapter, in which Raymond came across a painting of the Marchesa. He would study it, fascinated by her hypnotic beauty.

My mind strayed from my technical problem back to reality. In fiction, I could provide a convenient portrait for my protagonist. But in real life I had found nothing that would give me a likeness of Mirella's mother, the Contessa. If it was she I had seen that first night—and I still wasn't sure of it—she had been simply a shadowy silhouette. Since then, her image had been suggested only by its absence—in two empty plastic holders in a photograph album.

There had been nonvisual suggestions of her, though, of her presence in the house. Once, while lying in bed with Mirella, I had heard a faint sound from above us, a sound that might have been the creaking of a floorboard on the top story. Another time, after a session of lovemaking, when I had left the little bedroom to go to the bathroom, I had detected a strange scent in the hallway. It had been very faint, like a scent that had lingered after someone had passed through. Astringent and sweet, it could have been the fragrance of either a perfume or a medicine.

Then again I might have imagined the sound and the scent. It was a little disorienting for me to be constantly going back and forth between fiction and reality. It was possible that I was having some difficulty in separating the evidence of my senses from the products of my fancy.

There was no confusion at that moment, however. I was dealing strictly with fiction, and it was time to get on with my work. I concentrated again, composing my next paragraph. After a minute or two I had it.

Raymond recognized her at once. He remembered that face as he had seen it before, imbued with the artificial colors of the portrait painter.

But the face that confronted him was very pale, with an icy beauty that the artist had been unable to capture. The Marchesa Adelardi was now much older than the young woman who had posed for the portrait. But her bright gaze had lost none of its mesmeric quality. The haughty curve of her lip was as imperious as ever.

She stared at him for a long moment, as if she were committing him to memory. Then, with a stately sweep of her long dress, she turned and disappeared around the corner at the end of the gallery.

He did not follow her.

I had spent several weekends in a row at Mirella's country house. This weekend, however, I was to stay in the city to work on my book.

The writing had gone more rapidly than I had anticipated, and by Saturday night my chapter was finished. The next morning—a particularly beautiful morning—I found myself regretting my conscientiousness. I wished I were with Mirella, lazing away the day in the Connecticut sunshine.

I phoned her, but there was no answer. This wasn't too surprising; on such a perfect day, she wouldn't have stayed inside.

My impulse to be with her was stronger than ever, and there seemed to be no need to stand on ceremony. So I went out, rented a car—I could still be reckless with my credit cards—and drove up to Litchfield County.

I arrived at Mirella's place at a little past one. As I turned into her driveway, I saw that her car was parked in front of the house. This didn't necessarily mean that she was there, but at least she couldn't be far away.

I got out of the car and entered the house. There was no sign of her. "Mirella?" I called out.

There was silence for a moment. Then I heard Mirella's voice, calling down from the upper floor. "Carl?"

"That's right, sweetheart."

She appeared at the top of the stairway. She was wearing a shirt, fastened with one button, and seemingly nothing else.

"What are you doing here?" she asked.

"I couldn't stand being without you," I replied.

Mirella's smile, in response to this, was slow and sensual. She was, clearly, interpreting my need in only one way.

And, as I looked up at her, standing bare-legged on the top stair, her hair loose and uncharacteristically disheveled, I in fact felt a rush of desire that wiped out any other thought I might have had.

I ran up the stairs and took her in my arms. Her kiss was startling in its urgency; it was even more ravenous than mine. Her tongue filled my mouth.

I headed into the bedroom, pulling her after me. The bed was unmade, with the blankets heaped on the floor beside it, but I took no particular notice of this untidiness. I knew that Mirella was without her maid in the country. And, in my aroused state, I was aware of very little other than my hunger for her.

I stripped quickly and threw myself on her. She climaxed almost at once. She didn't relax at all, but went on straining at me, working toward still another orgasm.

I had never known her to be so completely abandoned. Her cries were ecstatic. I had started with the same wildness, but now, as we went on, I grew more tentative, uncertain. I had become conscious of something different, something strange, about this act of love. It wasn't simply her frenzy that was unusual; there was an actual tactile difference.

Her inner thighs had been moist and creamy from the beginning. She had been totally open, warm and lubricated. At one point, varying my angle of thrust, I briefly rolled onto my side and felt a pool of wetness on the sheet that couldn't have had anything to do with me, that had to have been there already.

I gave Mirella her additional orgasm, fused my own with it, then separated from her at once and lay on my back beside her. I was disturbed and suddenly very alert. I was seeking some sign that would confirm my unsettling suspicion.

Then I detected the slight acrid tang in the air, a faint smell I hadn't noticed at first: the leftover aroma of cigarette smoke. This was all the confirmation I needed; Mirella was a nonsmoker.

I rose to one elbow and looked into the ashtray that was on the bedside table, the ashtray that was kept there for my use. It was empty.

I got up from the bed.

"What are you doing?" Mirella asked.

I didn't answer. I went over to the wastebasket and looked down at it. I saw the cigarette butts she had dumped into it and an empty cigarette wrapper. A gold Dunhill wrapper. Larry Booth's brand.

I turned to Mirella. Her head was propped on a pillow and she was watching me.

"How long ago did Larry leave?" I asked.

Her expression changed, but only a little. She sat up, crossed her legs under her, and gazed at me calmly. "Ten minutes before you got here," she said.

"Was it good with him?"

"Yes. It was very nice."

Her tone was light and negligent, as if we were discussing some matter of minor consequence. I didn't know how I should interpret her casual manner. Was she adopting it as a pose to taunt me? Or was it, in fact, a genuine expression of her feelings?

If nothing else, it undercut me in my outrage, left me helpless. In the face of such a cool, civilized attitude, I couldn't vent my emotion without seeming to be foolishly overreacting. All I could do was go on asking questions—awkward but necessary questions.

"Was it the first time with him?" I asked.

She nodded. "The first time."

"But it won't be the last?"

"I don't know." Mirella pondered it for a moment, as if she wanted to be able to give me a more specific answer. Finally, she said, "Whatever I do, it doesn't concern *you*, Carl."

This was a little *too* cool for me, and I could no longer keep back my anger. "What the hell do you mean, it doesn't concern me?"

"If I meet an attractive man and I wish to go to bed with him," she said, "I will. It has nothing to do with you."

"It really has that little significance for you? You can fuck some guy—and then, a few minutes later, fuck me, too?"

"I had not *planned* it that way," she pointed out reasonably. "You turned up without warning."

"You didn't *have* to do it with me."

"No. But it was exciting." She smiled at me now. Her smile was without warmth; rather, it had a contemptuous lewdness to it. "And why are you complaining?" she asked. "You had a good time, didn't you?"

I stared at her, speechless for a moment. It was bad enough that she had put me in the humiliating position of the betrayed lover. But what made it unbearable was her deliberate slighting of my pain—her refusal to acknowledge that I even had a right to pain. It seemed to be not so much obtuseness as a perverse snobbery. It was as if she believed that only her equals could have delicate feelings—and I wasn't her equal.

At length I asked, "What kind of a woman are you, anyway?"

There was shock, and perhaps a little revulsion, in my voice, and her face went suddenly blank. Still, she shrugged casually as she said, "I am myself."

"And you see yourself as something pretty terrific, don't you?" The hurt and the rage was rising in me, feeding into each other. "The great lady—the Countess from Ferrara—the refined aristocrat who is so far above the rest of us peasants. Well, wake up, baby! Right now, as far as I'm concerned, you're nothing but a whore!"

Mirella's eyes widened. She rose from the bed and advanced on me, slowly, with such contained fury that I thought she might strike me. "How *dare* you speak to me that way?"

I stood my ground and met her glare directly; I wasn't going to let myself be intimidated by her. Still, my impulse—now that I had managed to arouse an emotional response in her—was to apologize.

"I'm sorry, Mirella," I said. "I didn't mean that—I shouldn't have said it. It's just that you get me angry. Couldn't you, at least, show some consideration for my feelings?"

But she was in no mood for an apology. The fury stayed alive in her eyes. "Why *should* I consider your feelings? What do you think you are—the great romantic man in my life? My lord, my master?"

"Maybe not," I said. "But I'm not your servant, either."

"No, you are something even lower than that." She smiled coldly. "Or have you forgotten, *caro?* You took money from me. You took money for sex. You are my paid lover, nothing else. So, which one of us is the whore?"

I just stared at her, stunned by the viciousness of it. It was as if she had indeed struck me—a disabling, unmanning blow that had left me sickened, helpless to defend myself.

Even at that moment, I recognized that there *was* no defending myself. She had turned an ugly truth on me. All I could do was stand mute, blinking in the sudden, stark light of self-recognition.

Finally, I voiced the words I had to say, the only words that could extricate me from this impossible situation, save me before I had degraded myself beyond any hope of self-respect.

"I'm not going to see you again."

17

Denny asked no questions. She accepted me back readily, unemphatically, without any real acknowledgment of the many months of separation. It was as if I had returned from a moderately lengthy business trip. We simply picked up where we had left off.

We started off our first evening back together with drinks at her apartment. The phone rang a couple of times, but in both cases Denny put off the party at the other end with a cool, "I'll call you tomorrow, all right?" I didn't pry, but I knew that she wouldn't have been so curt with another woman or a business associate. I felt sure that Denny now had two suddenly puzzled and unhappy gentlemen friends.

I took her out to dinner and then to a movie. It was a foolish Hollywood comedy, the kind of low-grade, eager-to-please product Mirella disdained. Denny and I, on the contrary, had always been aficionados of film schlock—as long as it had professionalism and energy, anyway—and we had a thoroughly good time.

When we returned to her apartment, she prepared some scrambled eggs, with a touch of curry powder in them, and crisp strips of bacon. Denny enjoyed fixing late-night snacks, and I found that my appetite for them was totally restored.

Through the course of all this, we had several hours of conversation. But I never brought up my affair with Mirella. And, after an initial probe to establish that it was all over, Denny didn't inquire about it.

Instead, I listened as she brought me up to date on our mutual friends—the friends who had vanished for me in my recent lost period. Life, I discovered, had gone on in its usual changeable way. A marriage had disintegrated, two new romances had started up, and someone had left for L.A.

Denny also gave me the latest gossip about the guests who appeared on the television talk show that employed her, and for once I listened to it with pleasure. Previously, it had irked me; I didn't share Denny's fascination with the messy personal lives of the so-called celebrities who were featured on the show. Most of them, I thought, didn't deserve more than passing attention. And, in the cases of those few who did, those who had made genuine contributions, I would rather not have known about their fornications and coke-snortings, or about their eccentric misbehavior in front of a camera.

But now, after the long months of my dark aberration, Denny's stories seemed like reports from a sane, sunlit world, a world in which open, amiable people made love and pleasured themselves in uncomplicated ways.

Finally, we went to bed, and the lovemaking was tender, replenishing. When I lay beside her afterward, I felt soothed by the comforting animal togetherness I had with her, felt myself being healed by it.

It wasn't until the next morning, when we were sitting over cereal and toast in her dining nook, that the black mood seized me again, gripped me with icy fingers. I had had a respite from it, but not, as it turned out, a very long one. It was less than forty-eight hours, after all, since I had left Mirella at her Connecticut house.

I put down my spoon, rose, and went into the living room. I sat on the couch and stared ahead. A minute passed, and then Denny was there, too, sitting across from me. Her expression was polite, as if she didn't want to intrude on my thoughts. But there was concern in her eyes.

At length, she asked, "Do you want to talk about it?"

I could have stalled, put her off. But Denny, I knew, would be departing for work soon. If I was to unburden myself at all, I would have to do it then and there.

And it might be beneficial, I thought, to let loose my disturbed thoughts in this cheerful, sunny apartment. In this environment, bright with Denny's ideas of decor—the Matisse and Miró reproductions, the profusion of pink, red, and orange throw pillows, the stuffed toy animals—what had seemed sinister might be rendered harmless, what had seemed threatening might be disarmed.

"I've had a new vision of myself," I said. "And I don't like it much."

I told her the whole story; or almost the whole story—I stopped short of the degrading endpoint in Mirella's Connecticut bedroom. I explained to her the reason I had entered into an affair with Mirella, how I had set out to write a novel based on the dramatic events that had taken place in her past. I told her how, in spite of the coolness and calculation of my motive, I had become obsessed with the woman, had found myself becoming a haunted, confused character, half observer and half participant, in some dark, mysterious story that was continuing on in the present.

"And then," I concluded, "last Sunday, I snapped out of it. It was like I had come up from some underground cave and was breathing fresh, clean air for the first time in months. And I could see clearly again. Suddenly, I saw what I had been doing—what I had been doing to myself."

Denny was smiling, obviously pleased by my description of my return to sanity. At the same time, she looked a little puzzled.

"That's great," she said. "But I don't understand. What happened that made you come to your senses?"

"Oh, it was nothing important. Just something that was said." I made little of that "something that was said"; I knew I could never repeat it to her, then or ever. "But it forced me to question myself. I mean, suddenly I wondered—was I doing what I was doing for the sake of a book? Or was I using the idea of a book as an excuse for doing it? Using art as a license to indulge the perverse, kinky things in myself?"

"I can't answer that," Denny said. "Since I don't know what you were doing." She paused. "And I don't think I *want* to know."

"And I don't want to tell you," I said. "Let's stick with this on the philosophic level."

"Let's," she agreed.

"Okay, then," I went on. "Is the writing of a novel—my kind of personal novel—in some way an act of prostitution?" I had returned to Mirella's contemptuous accusation, after all. But if I used it as a metaphor, I could deal with it. "Is a novelist just an excessively literate whore?"

Denny seemed a little taken aback. "That thought has never occurred to me."

"Then think of it. A novelist takes the most private, painful, shameful things in his life and reenacts them publicly. Isn't there something obscene about this? Is it a whole lot different from a live sex show?"

"Depends on the writing," she said.

It was a reasonable response, and, at one time, I would have settled for it. But now I wanted her to see beyond the common sense of it, to have some idea of the disturbing questions, so long buried, that had risen to trouble me.

"I used to say that art was amoral," I said. "That the novelist, the poet, the painter, should be free to express himself without restrictions—and that the work, if it was good enough, would justify anything. But why? Why should the novelist be any more free of moral considerations than the man who makes baby food or automobiles? Is what he's doing that important? Is there even a need for it? Aren't there enough made-up stories in the libraries already?"

She thought about it for a second, then shrugged. "You're doing it for yourself, I guess."

"Yes, for myself—in a way I still don't quite understand. In my practical moments, I tell myself I do it for the money. But the hooker says that, too. And she can be deluding herself. The truth may be that she needs to get off by debasing herself. Just as the novelist gets off by debasing himself."

Denny looked at me uncertainly. "What are you trying to say? That you don't want to go on with this book?"

"Oh, I'll go on with it. It's that old professional discipline. I've committed myself to it—so I'll finish. But I don't know if I'll ever do another one."

I paused and studied Denny's expression. It remained calm; she showed no shock at the idea. It occurred to me that, after all the time

I had known her, I still wasn't sure what importance my career had for her. She had always been sympathetic; but Denny was naturally sympathetic.

"What would you think," I asked, "if I stopped writing novels?"

"You'd be the same person to me," she replied, "no matter what you did."

"Then you think I could be rehabilitated?"

Denny smiled. "I'd make it my special project."

I was back in the pleasant, companionable round. On Wednesday evening, Denny and I had dinner with the Morgensterns at a Chinese restaurant they had discovered. The husband was an airline executive and fairly typical of his breed, but I had always felt an affinity for him, since he, too, hailed from the Pacific Northwest. The restaurant was only a moderate hit with me. It was so authentically Szechwan that my mouth was scorched for hours afterward.

Thursday evening we checked out the current trendy disco in the company of Chuck, one of Denny's co-workers on the television show, and his latest gorgeous girlfriend. Ordinarily, I would have excused myself from a disco excursion. But, in my new carefree mood I was game for anything.

Friday evening we went to a small party at Phil and Nancy's apartment. Phil and Nancy were the couple who, in the past, we had seen most often—mainly because they wore well. Nancy was so bright and witty that it was hard to believe that she was an ex-model. And Phil, an advertising hotshot who featured a Satanic look—a shaved head and a villainous black beard—happened to have the nature of a gentle, playful twelve-year-old boy.

We sang folk songs to Phil's guitar accompaniment. Most of them were chestnuts I had learned in my childhood, and I was hardly ever at a loss for a verse. Then we played charades. Pantomime wasn't normally my forte, but I was feeling so relaxed that I was suddenly inspired, and led my team to an easy victory.

When Denny and I were leaving, we made tentative plans with our host and hostess to spend a weekend with them at their place in Amagansett. "Don't be a stranger," Phil said to me, as we shook hands.

It was a conventional statement, but it had a special point for me. It struck me that I *had*, for a spell, become a stranger, not only to the people who cared for me, but to the world in general. I had taken on some of the coloration of the woman I had consorted with, had shared her alienation. Like her, I had moved warily in byways, keeping to the shadows.

I dropped Denny at her door. Her period had suddenly arrived, which ruled out sex for us. And I had had a little too much to drink anyway. I decided that I would rather spend the night in my own bed. It would be the first time I had done so that week.

When I got back to my apartment, I checked my answering machine. The red light was on; someone had called. I played back the tape. There were seconds of silence, then an audible hang-up. The person at the other end, I assumed, had debated leaving a message and decided against it.

I went into the kitchen and turned on the flame under the pot of leftover coffee. While the coffee was heating, I wandered into my study and looked down at my manuscript; just looked at it, I didn't touch it. I had avoided touching it all week. It was as if there were some contagion in the bond paper itself that might bring back my delirium.

But I knew I shouldn't be childish about it. It was a hundred-and-fifty-odd sheets of typing paper, nothing more; a bundle of technical problems waiting to be resolved. It was time to bring my little vacation to an end. I decided I would resume work the next morning.

I returned to the kitchen, poured a cup of coffee, and took a quick swallow of it. I didn't want to linger over it. I wanted just enough coffee to clear my head and then I would go to sleep—before I started coming down from my high, before the alcohol changed gears in my brain and plunged me into depression.

I heard the telephone ring.

I froze, with my cup suspended in midair. Immediately, I knew who it was; and it wasn't simply because it was past midnight and no one else—other than Denny, perhaps—would phone me that late.

The fact was, I had been expecting her call all week. It was overdue.

Still, I toyed with the idea of ignoring it. I stayed motionless for two rings. But then, when the phone kept on ringing, I put down my cup, quickly went out to the living room, and picked up the receiver. "Hello?"

"Are you alone?" Mirella asked, just as she had the first time she had ever called.

"What business is it of yours?" I snapped. Then I was instantly contrite, as I listened to the wounded silence at the other end of the line. "Yes, I'm alone," I said. "I'm about to go to bed." The silence continued. "How are you, Mirella?"

"Lonely," she said softly. "I miss you, Carl."

Angry replies came to my mind. I might have asked coldly, was it so difficult to find another paid lover? Was there no one else worth buying? But I didn't have the heart for any of the cutting rejoinders I had rehearsed in my imagination. The desolation in her voice was too genuine.

"I'm sorry," I said. "But I think it's best this way."

"Where were you tonight?" she asked.

"I was seeing some friends," I said..

After a moment, she said, "I didn't mean those things I said to you."

"You sounded convincing at the time."

"You got me angry. When I get angry, something bad in me comes out. It takes possession of me, I can't help it."

"You want to punish. I know."

"You are a fine man, Carl. An honorable man. I want you to know I really believe that."

These were flattering, soothing words. But they seemed a little stiff and insincere to my ear.

"Look," I said, "I only borrowed the money because I was in a bind. I'll pay it back to you. I promise. Every cent of it."

"Please don't talk about the money," she pleaded. "The money isn't important."

"You made an issue of it Sunday."

"I was wrong to do that," she said miserably. "I miss you so much, Carl." Wanly, she asked, "Don't you miss me at all?"

"A little," I admitted.

It was unwise of me to encourage her even this much. Mirella took it as her cue to change her approach. Her voice shifted to a sensual half-whisper.

"I need you, darling," she said. "I wish I were touching you—stroking you—feeling your body against mine. Don't you need me, too?"

"I don't think we should talk about it."

"I'm getting excited just hearing your voice. Do you know what I'm doing now, Carl? I'm touching myself. I'm wet."

I was helplessly silent now. In spite of myself, I was envisioning her as she was at that moment, with her smooth, white thighs parted, her fingertips dangling over the wilderness of dark pubic hair, teasing the glistening pink lips. And I felt a honeyed ache surge in my crotch.

"Don't you need me, too, Carl?" she asked again.

"I'm about to hang up, Mirella," I said.

"No! Don't hang up yet."

"It's late. I want to go to bed."

After a moment, Mirella said, "All right. But may I call you again?"

"I don't see what that would accomplish."

"It comforts me, darling. Just to be able to talk to you."

"Okay. But let's not talk any more now. Good night."

I hung up quickly.

I just stood there, looking down at the black instrument. It left me vulnerable, like a breach in a wall. At any untimely hour, it might ring, and Mirella, for a few moments at least, would have me again.

I thought of Sasha Rombeck suddenly. Mirella had used the phone to toy with Sasha's most shameful memories. I, too, had such memories now, as delicious as they were perverse. Mirella would not let me forget them.

18

The letter was written on Rutgers University stationery. The printed heading specified "Dept. of Political Science."

It was a stiff, formal note, cautiously worded. It said:

Dear Mr. Hopkins:

I am writing on behalf of Ann Walling.

Mrs. Walling will be in New York City next week and she would appreciate it if you would meet with her, at your convenience, to discuss a matter of great concern to her, and, quite possibly, of interest to you as well.

I will be phoning you shortly to arrange this meeting, if it is agreeable with you.

Sincerely,

Tari Anvari

I studied this letter perplexedly. Ann Walling, I assumed, was Tobias Walling's mother; though I couldn't be absolutely sure, since I had never learned his mother's first name. The "matter of great concern" most likely involved her late son. But why was she seeking *me* out?

The sender of the letter offered little information about this, and none about himself. I guessed from his name that he was Iranian; the only Tari I had known had been an Iranian fellow student at college. Judging by the letterhead, he worked at Rutgers; quite possibly he was a faculty member.

But what was his connection with Tobias's mother? Why was he serving as her intermediary?

I didn't have long to wait for the answers to some of these questions. The next morning Tari Anvari phoned me.

He had a light voice and the beautiful speech of a cultured native of the Third World. His foreignness showed mainly in the loving precision with which he articulated each English word.

He announced himself and then asked if I had received his letter. Yes, I told him, and I would be happy to talk with Mrs. Walling. He expressed his delight and asked if four o'clock on Monday afternoon, at the Hotel Carlyle, would be convenient for me. That would be fine, I told him.

"Now, can you tell me what this is all about?" I asked.

"I'm afraid I can't," he said. "Not on the phone."

"I suppose it has something to do with Tobias?"

"Yes, of course. But I can say no more than that. We'll explain when we see you."

"You'll be there, too?"

"Yes."

It was obvious that I wasn't going to find out anything more about this mysterious meeting. But, while I had him on the phone, I thought I might as well learn what I could about Tari Anvari.

"I noticed that you wrote from Rutgers," I said. "Are you a professor, Mr. Anvari?"

"An assistant professor."

"And your field?"

"The politics of the Middle East—as you might suspect."

"Should I be calling you Dr. Anvari?"

He laughed. "You could. But my father is Dr. Anvari, too. I feel more comfortable when people call me Tari."

I immediately took twenty years off his imagined face. I was talking to a young man, near the beginning of his academic career, and still a little insecure about his position.

"Are you a friend of Mrs. Walling?" I asked.

"Yes," he said. "But I was Toby's friend first."

I was struck by the fact that he referred to Walling as Toby. That was something that, as a rule, only Mirella did. The others in his circle had always called him Tobias.

"A close friend?" I asked.

"Very close," he replied. "I look forward to meeting you on Monday," he said suddenly. He was in a hurry to bring this conversation to an end now. "See you then."

The door was opened by a young man of startling good looks: a dark, lean face, large, liquid eyes, with only the beakiness of his nose as a deviation from the Western norm of beauty.

"You're Tari?" I asked.

"Yes," he replied. "Come in, Carl."

We had lost no time getting on a first-name basis, but he didn't shake the hand I offered. A glimpse at his right hand, as he gestured me into the room, revealed a possible reason why. It was strangely misshapen. It didn't seem to be a birth deformation; rather, it was as if every bone in the hand had been broken and it had healed poorly.

I entered the hotel room. A tall, white-haired woman, in a gray suit with a high-necked blouse, rose and came toward me.

"It's a pleasure meeting you, Mr. Hopkins," she said, holding out her hand. "I'm Ann Walling."

I murmured an appropriate response and bowed over her hand. Something courtly seemed to be called for. She wasn't just an old lady; she was a presence.

The only previous impression I had of her had come from Tobias's attempt at a novel, in which he had portrayed his mother—or the character based on her—as a sensual, passionate young woman. But the woman I saw now seemed beyond all passions, with no more warm movement in her than a glacial formation. She probably never had been beautiful. But in old age her face, which must have been too strong and bony for a girl, had settled into a mask, without gender, that compelled, that was commanding.

She stood before me now, as straight and stiff as a totem, her unblinking eyes holding me. Then, almost as if it was an afterthought, she said, "We have some tea. Would you like some?"

"Yes, thank you, I would," I replied.

She made no move to serve me. It was Tari who rushed over to the tea tray that was set up on a side table.

"Sit down, please," Mrs. Walling said.

I sat on the sofa. Mrs. Walling returned to the chair she had been sitting in, an armchair that was to one side of the sofa, facing the door.

Tari came back with two cups of tea, giving me one and placing the other beside Mrs. Walling. Then he pulled up a straight-backed chair and sat opposite me, on the other side of the coffee table. He crossed his legs, took a cigarette case from the inside pocket of his navy-blue suit, removed a cigarette, and lit it. He had no difficulty in using his maimed hand, I noticed; he flipped his lighter easily enough. But, after putting the lighter away, he kept the cigarette in his undamaged left hand and let his right hand sink onto his lap, where it rested mostly out of sight.

As I sipped my tea, I took in the room. It was, I supposed, one of the larger, more expensive rooms at the Carlyle. It was luxuriously furnished, and it had been brightened by bunches of carnations, situated in vases in three different places. The carnation, I assumed, was Ann Walling's favorite flower. A sweet fragrance had permeated the air of the room when I entered, but now it was being erased by the heavy aroma of Tari's Turkish tobacco.

The silence had extended for most of a minute. I decided that I might as well start the conversation myself.

"I don't know why you wanted to talk with me," I began. "I should point out that I didn't really know Tobias."

"We're aware of that," Mrs. Walling said.

"We know all of Toby's close friends," Tari said.

"And you are a stranger," Mrs. Walling said.

This didn't seem a particularly friendly note on which to begin. But I smiled agreeably and said, "Well, okay. Then why did you want to see me?"

"Because you do know Mirella Ludovisi," Mrs. Walling said.

"Yes, I know her."

"You know her very well." Pointedly, she added, "Intimately."

"No longer."

"We're aware of that, too," she said.

I was starting to get annoyed. This frosty old lady, whom I had never met before, was fixing me with steady blue eyes and addressing me about my most personal concerns. It didn't seem to dawn on her that she was being breathtakingly rude.

I tried to make a joke of it. "I hadn't realized that news of my love life had reached all the way to—Massachusetts, is it?"

She nodded. "Gloucester, Massachusetts."

"I'm the one who told Mrs. Walling, Carl," Tari said.

"Oh? And how do *you* know?" I asked.

"I had dinner with Alex Satin a little over a week ago," he said.

I should have guessed it would turn out to be Alex—the great leaky vessel for all of my secrets.

"All right," I said, "so, thanks to Alex, you know all about me." I looked at both of them. "But what do you want from me?"

"I'll get right to the point, Mr. Hopkins," Mrs. Walling said. Her voice was even, deliberate, with little variation in pitch. "Mirella Ludovisi murdered my son. We want to see that justice is done. And we want you to help us."

I took a moment to think over my answer. I wanted to be very careful. "First," I said, "I don't believe that's true. I don't believe Mirella murdered Tobias."

"But you're writing a novel about it," Tari said. "Alex told me."

"That is fiction. Fiction is fiction. People don't seem to understand that," I said, with some irritation. "Second," I went on, "even if it were true, why should *I* help you?"

"We were hoping we could appeal to your moral sense," Mrs. Walling said.

Perhaps I looked unimpressed, because Tari quickly offered another inducement. "And to your curiosity as a novelist," he said. "Alex told me that your affair with Mirella wasn't a real romance, that you were researching your novel. Well, you would learn much more if you cooperated with us."

Tari was no fool. He had seized upon the one reason I could be tempted, the reason, in fact, that I was remaining in that room.

Still, I felt I should further establish my basic disagreement with them. "I'm writing a novel about suspicion," I said, "not murder. Suspicion is very different from the fact of murder. And, frankly, in the case of Tobias's death, that's all that seems to exist—suspicion."

"We're going on more than just suspicion," Mrs. Walling said.

"You have evidence?"

"There are circumstances. Circumstances that can be explained only one way."

"Such as what?"

Mrs. Walling took a sip of her tea, slowly, as if she wanted time to think, to decide if I was worthy of her confidence.

Finally, her gaze met mine again. "Do you know about the changed will?" she asked.

"Yes, I've heard about that," I said. "But it doesn't prove that your son was murdered."

"No, perhaps not," she said. "Only an autopsy could prove that." She put down her tea cup. "Do you know why there was no autopsy, Mr. Hopkins?"

This gave me pause. I suddenly wondered why, indeed, Mrs. Walling hadn't ordered an autopsy? With her wealth and connections, she presumably could have overcome any official obstacles.

"No, I don't know," I replied.

"As soon as I learned of Tobias's death," she said, "or as soon as I recovered from the shock—I started to make arrangements. I sent a cable to Mirella, telling her that I would have the body shipped home to be buried in the family plot. She cabled me back immediately. It wouldn't be necessary for me to do anything, her cable said. She had already had Tobias cremated."

"Cremated!" I echoed.

"In Ferrara. The day after he died."

My astonishment was clear enough. But Tari jumped in now to drive home the point. "Do you realize how unusual that is in a Catholic country like Italy?" he asked. "Particularly with the people of Mirella's class? There surely had never been a cremation in her own family."

"I was left with only his ashes," Mrs. Walling said. "She finally let me have his ashes."

Her grief came through now; not as tears—her eyes remained dry and cold—but as a hardening of the mask that was her face.

I let a couple of seconds pass before I spoke again. "So you think he was poisoned?"

"Mirella met with Piers Allison," she said, "just before Tobias's death."

"Piers Allison, as I'm sure you know," Tari said, "is an expert nonpareil on rare drugs and poisons."

"Mirella told me about that meeting," I said. "They got together in Venice—and Tobias was with them."

"She could easily have found an opportunity to be alone with Allison," Mrs. Walling said.

"That's a supposition," I said.

She reacted to this with a slight tightening of her mouth. "Very well, then, Mr. Hopkins," she said, after a moment. "Why is Piers Allison blackmailing her?"

"*Is* he blackmailing her?" I instantly realized what she was referring to. "She lent him some money. But Mirella is generous with her friends."

"She has given him several sums of money."

"How do you know that?"

"I have had a private investigator working on this."

"Oh?" I glanced at Tari, then looked back at Mrs. Walling, wondering now if Alex Satin had been their only source of information about me. "And have I appeared in this man's reports?"

"In a sketchy way, yes," Mrs. Walling said.

"It's the reason I had that dinner with Alex," Tari said, with a smile.

The idea of this private eye intrigued me. He could have been my point-of-view hero, if I had been writing another kind of novel. "Did you send this detective to do an investigation in Italy?" I asked.

145

"No," Mrs. Walling replied. "I used Italian investigators for that purpose. A firm in Milan."

"You've gone to great expense, I see."

"Tobias was my only child," she said. There was no sentiment in her tone; her voice remained calm and unwavering, as if she were stating a diamond-hard reality. "He was my reason for existence when he was alive. He continues to be my reason to exist now that he is dead."

Her hunger for vengeance, I sensed, was an even more intense vital force than her mother love. It could keep her keen until she was a hundred.

"What about Mirella's mother?" I asked. "Have your investigators found out anything about her? Or aren't you interested in the Contessa?"

"We're *very* interested in her," Mrs. Walling said. "Particularly since she had a great influence over Mirella." Meaningfully, she asked, "And may have continued to have an influence over her."

"But she was in a mental hospital for years."

"Not at the time of Tobias's death. She had escaped by then. With Mirella's help."

Once again, I was surprised. "Mirella arranged the escape?"

"Mirella was on a visit to Italy. The Contessa was confined in a mental hospital near Viareggio. My investigators have established that Mirella was in that neighbourhood at the time of her mother's escape. Very probably, she bribed a hospital attendant."

"Where is the Contessa now?" I asked. "Have your Italian detectives found that out?" Casually, I added, "Or your man here?"

"No," she replied. "No one knows where she is."

I could have possibly enlightened them on this point, could have told them I thought I knew the answer. But I saw no reason as yet why I should be helpful. Anyway, I too was simply going on a presumption—powerful though my suspicion was.

"All right," I said. "Everything you've told me is very interesting. But what do you want me to do?"

Neither of them said anything for a moment. Then Tari smiled at me. His smile, when he flashed it, was warm and charming. "We gather that you've had a falling out with Mirella," he said. "It was nothing serious, I hope?"

"Serious enough so that I don't want to see her again."

"Perhaps you're being too inflexible," he said. "We think you *should* start seeing her again."

"Why?"

"You might find out something."

"Something that would nail down your case against her?"

"That would make her answer for her crime," Mrs. Walling said.

"And you want me to go back to sleeping with this woman so I can help you hang her?" I asked, a bit incredulously.

"What you do with her is your own business," Tari said smoothly. "All we're asking is that you resume contact with Mirella."

I just looked at them for a moment, these two obsessed people who could be so bald-faced in their eagerness to use me.

"Why do you expect me to do this?" I asked. "My moral sense?"

"Yes," Mrs. Walling said. "And, if you wish, there would be a financial reward."

It was the wrong thing to say—I had been accused of being a whore too recently—and I felt my face harden.

Tari quickly spoke up to repair the damage. "Carl isn't interested in money," he said to Mrs. Walling. "He's a very respected novelist, you know. All he cares about is his work." This bit of oblique flattery accomplished, he turned to me again. "And, Carl, what you might learn now would give you a better book."

"If I do as you suggest," I said, after a moment, "it will be for only one reason. To establish the truth. The truth might turn out to be different from what you suspect."

"We would be happy to discover that," Tari said.

I rose. "However," I said, "I can't decide anything now."

"We didn't expect you to," Tari said, rising also. "We just wanted to let you know our thoughts on the matter."

"I'm sure you'll do the right thing, Mr. Hopkins," Mrs. Walling said. "For Tobias's sake," she added, more softly, as if her son's troubled spirit were hovering nearby. "We mustn't forget Tobias."

She seemed very tired now. She didn't rise when I took my leave of her.

Tari accompanied me out and went down in the elevator with me. We said little during the descent, since we weren't alone; a well-dressed couple was standing beside us.

When we came out into the lobby, Tari stopped and said, "I hope Mrs. Walling didn't offend you."

"Not at all," I replied.

"This has become a monomania with her. It can make her a little insensitive to other people."

"Yes, she *is* a single-minded lady. But you seem pretty caught up in this, too," I commented. "Tobias must have meant a lot to you."

"I owed everything to him," Tari said. "My career. My life."

"Your life?"

"I was one of Toby's good deeds. He rescued me from the Shah's prison."

"How did that happen?"

"He knew my father, through his scholarly work. My father is a great student of Persian art and history—as Toby was. Toby learned from him that I was a political prisoner. He campaigned relentlessly, went to the highest authorities—until I was released and allowed to immigrate to this country."

"Would they have executed you?"

"Who knows?" he said, with a shrug. "But I don't think I would have survived." He held up his ruined hand. "The Savak were not gentle."

I said nothing now. "I should get back to Mrs. Walling," Tari said, after a moment. "I hope we'll be seeing you again, Carl."

"I can't guarantee it."

"I realize that." He paused. "Pursue the truth, Carl. That's all we ask—that you pursue the truth."

When I returned to my apartment, I thought about Tari's parting words. There had been an ambiguousness to them. He had urged me to pursue the truth, as if it were an elusive, difficult quarry. It occurred to me that Tari might not perceive it as being the clear-cut thing it was to Mrs. Walling. He was giving his benefactor's mother whatever assistance she asked from him. But it was possible that he viewed Tobias's death and the circumstances surrounding it in much the same way that I did, as suspicious—particularly the hasty cremation—suggestive of sinister possibilities, but also explicable in terms of the unpredictable workings of natural disease and human behavior. Ann Walling wanted Mirella's head, but Tari might simply have wanted an answer.

I wanted an answer, too; several answers. And it wasn't simply that I felt I should try to exonerate Mirella, dispel the cloud of suspicion that hung over her. I was no private eye, like the operatives Mrs. Walling had hired. While I had a streak of gallantry in me, cared for Mirella, and was moved by her predicament, it still made more sense for me to stay out of the situation.

But I was a novelist whose work-in-progress had suddenly gone sour. I had returned to my manuscript, had been putting in daily stints on it, and almost everything I wrote seemed lifeless, false. My wastebasket was filled with crumpled, discarded pages. It was as if, cut off from direct contact with the source of my inspiration, I had no talent for the subject, as if my imagination was dead.

I had learned too little, had stored up too few impressions; I didn't have nearly enough to carry me through the course of a whole novel. I needed to know more, to experience more. Much more.

Anyway, I hadn't been able to exorcise Mirella from my thoughts. She had made sure of that by phoning me again and again, tantalizing me in some new way each time. I had resisted her, remonstrated with her, but I had allowed each phone conversation to go on a little longer than was necessary.

Now I had two reasons to see her, Mrs. Walling's request and my own artistic needs. But even without these reasons, I suspected, it would have come to the same thing. Deep within me I had known all along that, sooner or later, I would have to be with her again.

19

At the door Mirella embraced me hungrily. I was careful in my response. I kissed her on the cheek and quickly separated from her. I stepped back to arm's length, said something conventional about how beautiful she was looking, and then walked into the living room.

I glanced around; there was no one in sight, no sound came from the rest of the house. It was either Porfiria's day off or Mirella had instructed her to stay out of the way during our reunion.

Mirella was subdued now and tentative. She could sense from my manner that, whatever was about to happen with us, it would in some way be different from before—or at least that I intended it to be different. She offered me a drink as politely as if I were visiting there for the first time. I asked for a Perrier water; I wanted to have a clear head for what I was about to say.

At length, when we were settled down with our glasses of mineral water beside us, I said, "I didn't expect ever to come here again."

"I didn't know," she said. "But I prayed." She smiled now; her smile had some of the wonderment of thanksgiving. "And you are here."

I had never heard her refer to praying before. It hadn't occurred to me to even wonder if she was religious. She was, I realized now, but in some very basic Catholic way; a primal faith that was beyond articulating.

"You are no longer angry with me?" Mirella asked.

"I was never really angry with you," I said. "I was angry with myself—because of the position I'd let myself get into."

"We won't talk about that," she said. "Let's forget about that. "It's not important." She gazed at me, with a sudden fervor in her eyes. "I love you, Carl."

I was startled. "Love" wasn't a word that had come up in our conversations—not as a term that was applicable to our relationship, anyway. I wasn't entirely sure what she meant by it.

I stared at her rather stupidly and said, "You didn't have to say that. I mean, I didn't come here to make you say that."

"It's what I feel. It has taken me this long to realize it. But now I know. So why can't I say it?"

"Because I'm not asking you to love me now. I want you to be my—" I broke off, unable to utter the lame phrase.

A bitter smile of realization came onto her face. "Your friend?"

"Yeah. My friend."

"Is it that you have someone else to love now?" She paused. "Denise?"

"Denny, yeah," I admitted. "I've been seeing her again."

"I understand."

We were silent now. It was, I supposed, a painful silence for her, and it was an awkward one for me; I was already regretting being there. But I had made my decision, I had to go through with it.

"I've missed you, Mirella," I said. "I've missed you a lot. And I don't see why, just because I've gone back to Denny, we have to deprive ourselves completely of the pleasure of each other's company. I should feel free to come visit you—go out with you—just as I would with any friend."

I knew that this was the idiotic kind of thing caddish ex-lovers had been saying over the centuries in the same situation. But in my case I was trying to be fair and honorable. I was ready to "pursue the truth" again. This time, though, I didn't want to take sexual advantage of her.

"You want to make life easy for yourself, I see," Mirella commented dryly.

"Why not?" I asked. "Why should either of us be childish about it? Isn't it better that we see each other as friends than that we don't see each other at all?—that we go on just having weird phone conversations late at night?"

151

"It's better, I suppose," she said. "Phone fucking isn't, finally, very satisfying."

I was a little taken aback, as I always had been whenever Mirella had unexpectedly come out with a sexual vulgarism. But there was no romantic pretense about her now. She was gazing at me coolly, with the sensual woman's unsentimental, sour understanding of men. It was as if she were seeing through me, recognizing the hollowness of everything I was saying.

I was beginning to recognize it, too, the emptiness of my insistence on a comradely friendship. Mirella wasn't wearing a bra and her blouse was fastened only by a lower button. It was carelessly open, revealing a portion of one breast. I couldn't keep my eyes away from the curve of tempting flesh.

"But, if we're going to be friends," I went on, "we have to be open with each other. There shouldn't be mysteries—secrets—coming between us."

"I have been honest with you," she said.

"Have you?"

"I have told you everything about myself."

"Not quite," I said. "I think you've kept one thing from me."

"What?" she asked.

I hesitated, then decided it was best to say it boldly, confront her with it swiftly, before she had time to get up her defenses.

"Your mother is here, isn't she? In this house?"

All expression vanished from her face. For a moment her eyes were totally alert, intense in their concentration on me. But she showed no agitation, or even much in the way of surprise.

"Yes," she said, finally.

"Oh. Well, then—" Now I was the one who was caught unprepared. I hadn't expected her to admit it so quickly and easily. "I've suspected it all along," I said. "I've sensed she was here. I even thought I saw her once."

"Very possibly you did," Mirella said calmly.

"Has she been here every time I've been here?"

"Always."

"Then you should have told me before. You should have trusted me."

"I wanted to trust you, Carl. But I didn't dare. I can't let myself trust anyone, not when it concerns my mother's freedom and well-being." She said this last phrase with simple gravity, as if it were the most important and sacred thing in her life. "They are hunting for her," she went on, "all over the world. Interpol has alerted every police force. If the authorities discovered that my mother was living in this house, she would be arrested, she would be extradited. They would send her back to Italy"—her face darkened—"to that terrible hospital. That is no place for someone like my mother. She belongs here with me."

She stated this with absolute conviction, and I wasn't inclined to argue the point with her. "I never would have betrayed you," I said.

"Perhaps not. And I'm glad you know now," she said, her tone lightening. "I will not have to be so—so constrained with you."

"That will be a blessing."

She smiled. Her look was almost teasing. "My mother has been very interested in you."

"Oh?"

"Would you like to meet her?"

She asked it casually, as if she were proposing the most ordinary social encounter.

"Now?" I asked.

"Yes, now."

"All right."

"Wait."

Mirella rose and left the room. I heard her go up the stairs. I sat where I was, sipping the Perrier water to ease the dryness in my throat. I knew that there was probably nothing to fear, but I was suddenly very nervous.

After three or four minutes had passed, Mirella came back down the stairs. She stood in the doorway and said, "It's all right. Mama says she would very much enjoy meeting you."

I rose and joined Mirella at the foot of the stairs. "She's on the top floor," she said. "You can go up by yourself. She wants to see you alone."

I looked at her questioningly. Mirella's faint smile was set, her expression unreadable. It was clear that she had told me as much as she felt necessary; I was to find out the rest on my own.

I went up the stairway to the next floor, the third floor of the house. I paused in a hallway that ran between the two bedrooms, hesitating uneasily, looking uncertainly at the last flight of stairs that led up to the top floor. Then I completed the turn and started up the stairs.

I had thought that the darkness at the top of the house might have been something of an optical illusion. But, when I came up onto the landing, I found myself in an actual darkness. It wasn't pitch-black; I could make out the structure of the floor. Rather than being broken up into several smaller rooms that were entered from a hallway, as the floor below was, this top floor consisted of two quite large rooms that opened into each other. I was standing by a wide archway that connected the two. The windows had been totally curtained off, and I could locate them only by the glints of light here and there, that managed to get through. There was an uncovered skylight nearby. I couldn't see it—it was on the other side of the archway—but there was a focused shaft of light coming down, creating a pale square on the floor. It was early evening now and the light was weak. It gave no illumination; it simply made everything around it seem darker.

The air was close and it had a clinging, fetid warmth. The peculiar scent was distinct in it, that scent I had detected once before, in the hallway below, as a faint, dying trace—a scent that had seemed half floral and half medicinal. It suggested its nature more specifically now: perfumed decay.

I glanced around, wondering in which direction I should go.

"In here," a woman's voice said.

The voice had come from the room on the other side of the archway. I turned and, stepping slowly, passed through the archway.

I was entering what seemed to be a sitting room. The chairs and tables were indistinct, but they had the bulkiness of furniture in a Victorian parlor. And there was another smell in the air now. Candle wax. Candles had been burning recently. But none were lit now.

"Stop there," the voice said. "Come no closer."

I stopped and peered through the murkiness at the woman who was sitting in a high-back chair by the far wall. I could make her out only as a silhouette. I could see that she was sitting very straight, very still, and that she was wearing a long dress that covered her to her ankles. But her face was a pool of shadow.

"Stay there, please," she repeated.

There was a silence. I realized now that I was standing under the skylight, illuminated by the shaft of light, and that the Contessa was studying me.

At length, she spoke again, but she was speaking to herself now. "Yes," she said softly. "Yes."

I was puzzled by what I heard in her voice, a strengthening certainty, a satisfaction. Then I remembered a photograph I had seen in Mirella's album, of Mirella's father with Gianfranco, the Contessa's lover. A face that had resembled my own had looked up at me from that photograph. I wondered if that was who the Contessa was seeing now—Gianfranco, the man she had murdered.

"You have been away a long time," the Contessa said. Her Italian accent was more pronounced than Mirella's, and she spoke slowly, with care, as if she was thinking out the words before she said them. "We have been waiting for you to return."

"There was a misunderstanding, Contessa," I said.

"You made my daughter very unhappy," she said. "She has cried."

"Well, I'm here," I said. "Mirella and I are going to be friends again."

There was another silence. It occurred to me that the Contessa might be as skeptical as her daughter about the possibility of innocent friendship between a sensual man and woman.

"I knew you would return," she said, finally. "I told Mirella that. I told her you would come back."

"How could you be so sure?" I asked.

"Because that is your destiny—to be with Mirella."

A chill went through me. It wasn't simply what she had said; in other circumstances, it might have been thought of as a figure of speech. But not here in this oppressive darkness. Uttered by that low, tired, haunted voice, the word "destiny" took on a special weight. I felt awe, as I would have in the cave of an oracle.

"We have been too long without a man," the Contessa said. "Women without a man—that is no family. The time has come for you to be what you must be. The man in the family."

I didn't know what to say, particularly since I couldn't be entirely sure she was speaking to me rather than her dead lover. My eyes were beginning to adjust to the darkness, and I squinted at her, hoping to make out her features. But she remained a shadowy figure, without a face.

"May I ask you something, Contessa?"

"Yes."

"Are you happy here?"

I asked the question almost without thinking; I hadn't intended to pry into her situation. But, as a humane impulse, I wanted to make sure that all was well with her in her strange confinement.

I sensed the Contessa's surprise. "Why do you ask that? It is not important," she said, "if I am happy. I am where I must be—with my daughter. It is my place. I belong with her." She paused. "You, too. You belong here."

Her voice had weakened on these final words, as if she had expended the last of her strength in saying them. When she spoke again, it was in a whisper. "Go back down now. Go back to Mirella."

I said nothing further, no polite parting words, no goodbye. I felt disoriented and confused, as if I had suddenly realized I was in a dream and yet couldn't awake. I simply turned, walked out of the room, and started back down the stairs.

Mirella was waiting for me in the hallway below. She was standing at the foot of the stairs, looking up at me as I descended. Her eyes were glowing, her lips were parted, and her beauty was like some overwhelming force of gravity, pulling me down toward her.

As I reached the last step, she stretched out her arms to me. I fell into her embrace, lost myself in it.

PART THREE

20

From then on I was part of the life at the East Eighty-fourth Street house. The house had a special interior life, I discovered, one I hadn't noticed in my previous, carefully monitored visits. Mirella had her daily routine, which I was only now beginning to comprehend, and there was a continuing flow of activity that emanated from the bottom floor, Porfiria's domain.

Porfiria was a Cuban, and she had numerous friendships, it seemed, in the Cuban exile community in nearby Spanish Harlem, just above East Ninety-sixth Street. Porfiria was a convivial sort, with her own people, anyway, and her friends would regularly come down to Yorkville to pass part of the day or the evening with her. There were two or three women of her own age, her personal friends; and then there was her boyfriend, Wilfredo—who was eight or ten years her junior—and *his* buddies. They would watch television in Porfiria's room, or sit around the large kitchen, eating, drinking, and chattering in energetic Spanish. Porfiria was as generous a hostess as her mistress, and she did not stint on the food and wine.

It was Mirella's food and wine, of course, but there was a payback for it. The house, like all old houses, was frequently in need of repair. Mirella, however, never found it necessary to send out for help, and, as I now knew, she had good reason to avoid having strange workmen poking about her house. There was all the manpower she needed in Porfiria's little circle. Wilfredo and his friends were always available. If they knew Mirella's secret, it was evidently safe with them. On the one or two occasions when, to be sociable, I drank wine with them in the kitchen, I got the impression that they, too, were living on the other side of the law. As a matter of general principle, they kept their distance from the police.

Wilfredo was a lean, mustached man with kinky hair and skin a shade darker than the Hispanic norm. He bore a scar on his neck and, most of the time, a challenging smile on his lips. He seemed tougher than his buddies, and they obviously looked up to him. I suspected that the trip to this country in the boat flotilla hadn't changed the nature of his life very much, that he had been the same thing in Havana that he was here—a thug. His manner spoke of violent crimes—armed robberies and drug-related murders.

It seemed odd that Porfiria, who was as respectable as any lady's maid, would have become romantically involved with such a sinister type. But then they shared their exile, and exile, I supposed, made strange bedfellows. In fact, exile was what everyone who moved about that house, with the exception of myself, had in common. It may have been the unspoken bond between Mirella and her mother and their Cuban helpers.

Menacing though he could be, Wilfredo seemed content to be the handyman at the house. With the help of his friends, he cleared out the basement of the accumulated junk of decades. And he performed the lighter tasks of repair by himself. His desire to be useful may have stemmed from his love for Porfiria—if that, indeed, was what he felt for her. And it may have had something to do with the fact that he seemed to be genuinely impressed by Mirella. He was as deferential with her as any medieval serf would have been with the lady of the manor.

His respect for the lady didn't extend to the lady's lover, as he revealed to me in various small ways. He made it particularly evident when I tried to assist him in the repair of a light switch.

I had volunteered to help out, which proved to be a mistake. I demonstrated quickly enough that I wasn't very good with my hands. Also that I was fearful around electrical currents.

Wilfredo thrust his screwdriver into the live fixture, touching off a shower of sparks. He looked at me and, with his eyes wide with challenge, asked, "Could you do that?"

I admitted that I lacked the nerve.

Wilfredo kept the sparks flying as he regarded me with the scornful smile of a macho male who was unafraid of electricity, who knew how to satisfy a woman, who could face down an enemy.

I pretty much had the run of the house now—all of it, that is, except the top floor. I didn't see the Contessa again. She kept to her gloomy quarters, living in her perpetual night.

But she wasn't, it seemed, a total shut-in. Once or twice a week, Mirella told me, in the late evening, the Contessa would go out for a walk in the neighborhood. She said that her mother preferred to be alone on these excursions. Perhaps, I thought, it briefly gave her the sense of being a normal person, an anonymous pedestrian observing the nocturnal life of the great city.

However, it couldn't alter the fact of her extreme isolation. There were just two people who occasionally kept her company, with whom she could talk. Mirella saw her every day, of course. Otherwise, her only companion was Porfiria. The maid took care of the Contessa's every need. And it wasn't done simply as part of her job; she devoted herself wholeheartedly to the task. Porfiria—so I was told—adored the Contessa.

I now understood how completely Mirella's life revolved around her mother. Mirella was, by nature, physically energetic, as evidenced by her fierce jogging every morning, and by her equally fierce shopping sprees some afternoons, when she would move restlessly from boutique to boutique, buying on impulse, buying things she wasn't likely every to wear. She was a woman who was meant to be out and around in the city, or exploring other parts of the world. And yet, after each brief foray, she would go directly home and remain there. When we went out together in the evening to a restaurant, we wouldn't wander around afterward, or go on to my place—Mirella had yet to see where I lived. We always returned to her house. I now realized why. Her mother was never out of her thoughts; she constantly had to make sure that all was well with her.

The situation was clearly very hard on her, though she never complained about it. The strain showed only in the furrow between her eyebrows; it had been slight when I had first met her, but it had deepened in the months since. I suspected now that she had bought the house in Connecticut from some desperate need for respite. It gave her the excuse to temporarily escape her mother and the darkness in the East Eighty-fourth Street house. But, still, she always came back in a day or so.

When she was home in New York, Mirella passed the time quietly. She was a reader, chiefly of popular fiction. Mine wasn't the only novel she had read in the past year; the best-sellers were stacked high in her bedroom.

Sometimes she would do nothing at all. She would curl up on the couch and stare vacantly, for long periods of time, lost in visions she didn't reveal to me or anyone.

I didn't discover this about her until I became a part-time resident at her house, spending as much of the day and night there as at my own apartment. Then, moving about the house, I would occasionally come upon her in the living room or bedroom, deep in one of her trances. It puzzled me at first; but soon I found out the reason—and it shocked me as much as anything I had learned about her.

Mirella took drugs.

I was so innocent about such things that I hadn't even suspected it. Then one evening when Mirella and I were undressing in the small bedroom—we still made love in this room rather than in the master bedroom—she disappeared, then returned, carrying a small vial of white powder. She asked me to try it. She told me that I should put a pinch of the powder on my tongue, let it dissolve, and then swallow it. She demonstrated it for me, doing it herself.

"What is it?" I asked warily, as I took the vial from her. "Cocaine?"

"Nothing that ordinary, darling," she said. "This is magic. It raises you to a higher level of existence. You feel beautiful. Everything seems beautiful."

"Where did you get it?"

"Piers gave it to me."

"What's it called?"

"He told me," she replied, with a shrug. "But I don't remember."

I didn't believe her; I guessed that for reasons of her own she was keeping the nature of the substance from me. This, of course, only added to my hesitation. But Mirella was insistent that I share the experience with her, if only this once. Finally, I gave in; I agreed to try it, on an experimental basis.

I put a pinch of the stuff on my tongue, wondering uneasily as I did so what I was about to ingest—powdered toad? essence of fly agaric mushroom? It was faintly bitter, but no more so than aspirin, and it went down easily enough.

It acted upon me quickly, and I was plunged into a maelstrom of sensations, tossed about in it seemingly for most of the night—except that, when I came out of it, only an hour had passed. And I couldn't recall much of it. I was left with only vague memories: of complex geometric patterns that had emerged from the surrounding matter, perceived in dazzling shades of color; of moving in some new dimension, without weight and with limitless extension; of sexual pleasure so intense that it had made me scream with astonished laughter.

When it was over, Mirella was pleased with the way the experiment had gone. But I was frightened. I never took that white powder again.

After that, I was concerned for Mirella; I worried about her health and sanity. I suspected now that what I had taken to be her natural dreaminess, what I had accepted as an intriguing unpredictability in her behavior, was, in large part, the result of drug-induced derangement. And she could have been involved with some very heavy drugs, indeed. Through Piers Allison, a whole magic barrel was available to her of some of the most exotic, mind-blowing potions in the world.

I wondered what other drugs she might have been using. My speculation ran the gamut from standard dope to the most bizarre substances, but actually the only other drug I ever encountered in that house was of a more mundane variety—though it certainly was one of the most dangerous.

I found it when I was helping Wilfredo with another repair job. We were trying to fix a cabinet door in Mirella's bathroom, which adjoined the master bedroom. The hinges of the door had sprung; in part because the wood had warped, but also because there had been pressure from the overstuffed shelves within the cabinet.

I removed a stack of large towels that had been overflowing the top shelf. They obviously hadn't been used in years; they were yellowed with age. I tried to think of some place where they could be temporarily stored.

It occurred to me that there might be room at the rear of Mirella's walk-in closet. I went into her bedroom, entered the closet, and checked the area at the back of it. A sheet was thrown over some object that was on the floor. Curious, I pulled back the sheet and saw that it was covering a metal foot locker.

I opened the foot locker and peered into it. I saw a row of squat pill bottles; perhaps a dozen of them. Each one was filled with red capsules.

I recognized the capsules immediately. Seconal.

I closed the foot locker, covered it again with the sheet, and put the stack of old towels on top of it. When I returned to the bathroom, I said nothing to Wilfredo about what I had found.

Still, I was troubled. The size of this hidden supply indicated much more than normal use; it was the cache of an addict. But it was hard to believe that Mirella was a barbiturate junky. I had known a couple of these unfortunates and I was familiar with the symptoms— slurred speech, unsteady balance. Mirella showed none of the usual signs. It was possible, of course, that she was managing to conceal them; I was well aware of her steely self-control.

But why would she need such a drug? I could understand why, sensualist that she was, she would be tempted by the hallucinogen we had shared, with its aphrodisiac side effects and its payoff in euphoria. But why would she, at the same time, crave a powerful downer that blanked out all sensations? Was her anxiety so great? I wondered.

Another possibility occurred to me—and, after what Mrs. Walling and Tari had told me, I was forced to consider it. It could be that she was trying to wipe out the pain of something deeper and more rending than mere anxiety.

Guilt.

Piers Allison was still around; he came by the house two or three times a week.

It wasn't that he was made to feel particularly welcome now. Mirella had perceptibly cooled toward him. She was increasingly restless in his presence; sometimes, she was openly hostile.

Piers didn't seem to notice. He would turn up, as cheerful as ever, and settle down comfortably with the insouciance of someone who was gifted with supreme obtuseness; or—if Mrs. Walling and Tari were correct in their surmise—with the self-confidence of the extortionist.

It seemed to me that he was staying on in New York rather a long time for a scientist-adventurer who specialized in primitive cultures. I asked him about it. Had he succumbed to the pleasures of city life? I inquired.

Piers laughed at the idea. *"What* pleasures?" he asked. "There's no joy in this city. It's worse here than in any jungle I've been in. At least, in the Yucatan, I know where I stand, I know the territory. I'm ready for anything that jumps out at me. Here I'm just a timid English tourist. I walk these streets, wondering which one of your crazed welfare cases is going to cut my throat. Give me the state of nature any time, old chum!"

"So, okay," I said. "When are you going back out into the field?"

"When I raise the money. That's what I'm trying to do now."

"Does it take a lot?"

"Enough. Mucking about in the wilderness can be expensive, you know."

This brief interchange between us took place when he was departing one evening. It was, at that point, our longest recent conversation, for I hadn't yet managed to have an extended talk with him alone.

That opportunity eventually presented itself, on a hot, sunny afternoon, when the three of us were sitting out in the garden, enjoying a bottle of chilled white wine. Mirella, for some reason, seemed annoyed with Piers—though he was being pleasant and inoffensive—and she contrived an excuse to disappear into the house.

Piers and I were sitting in wrought-iron garden chairs, with the bottle of wine on a low glass table between us. I didn't know how long we would be left alone, so I decided I should get directly to the subject I had always wanted to pursue with him.

"Tell me, Piers," I asked suddenly, "did you know Tobias well?"

He seemed a little startled by the question. "Didn't really know him at all, actually," he replied. "Met him just once."

"Where?"

"In Venice. Just before he died."

This, of course, checked out with the story Mirella had told me. But I pretended I was learning about it for the first time.

"You saw him just before he died?" I asked.

"Less than twenty-four hours before. He and Mirella had lunch with me."

"Did he seem sick to you?"

"Not at all. He seemed perfectly healthy. A very pleasant fellow, full of life. Had no idea he'd conk off that night. You never can tell about these things, can you?"

I was studying Pier's expression, but I could detect nothing that would lead me to believe that he might be an accomplice in murder. There were no signs of guilt or of any discomfort in discussing this topic. He showed nothing but the open-faced distress that any decent, sensitive person might have felt when reminded of an acquaintance's untimely death.

"Did you hit if off with Tobias?" I asked.

"Marvelously," he said. "We were friends at once. Of course, I felt I knew him already. Mirella had told me all about him."

"She had? When?"

"Oh, I passed through New York this time last year. I got together with Mirella. She unburdened her heart to me. Told me everything about her great new love, Tobias."

I had gone as far as I could with this line of questioning. I sat back, took a sip of wine, and glanced around the garden, as I tried to think of a new approach. The garden was contained by high walls. Geraniums and snapdragons were centrally located in it; beds of ivy bordered it all around.

"Lovely garden," I said, at length.

"Yes, beautiful," Piers said.

"I suppose Tobias did this all."

"I imagine so." After a moment, he added, "Though I think Tari put in the beds of ivy."

I stared at him. *"Tari* did?"

"According to Mirella."

"You know Tari?"

"Only from what Mirella has told me about him."

He had brought up Tari's name casually, as if he assumed that Mirella had talked about him. In fact, she had never mentioned him.

"When did Tari put in the ivy beds?" I asked.

"When he lived here," he answered.

"Tari lived here?"

Piers looked at me uncertainly now. "You didn't know that?"

"No, I didn't," I said. "When did he live here?"

"After Tobias got out of the hospital. Tari took care of him here."

"Why was Tobias in the hospital?" I was suddenly hopeful that a natural, acceptable explanation for Tobias's death might be at hand. "A heart condition?"

"No," Piers said. His manner had become guarded. "He was sick another way."

"What other way?"

Piers looked to his side. His hearing was sharper than mine and he had detected Mirella's almost noiseless approach. She was standing near us now, glaring at Piers, her eyes cold and her smile dangerous.

"You have said enough, Piers," she said. "Don't you think so? You have no business talking about those things."

Piers did his best to maintain his dignity. "I have a perfect right to say whatever I wish."

"What gives you that right?" Mirella asked angrily. "What gives you the right to gossip about the dead?"

"Gossip? We were talking about the garden, love, that's all."

"You were telling him stories."

"Not exactly." He cocked his head and smiled at her. "But I *could* tell stories, couldn't I, Mirella?"

Mirella was silent for a moment. Then, very quietly, she said, "You are starting to bore me, Piers. I think it's time for you to go away."

"I will go away," he said. "Just give me what I need for my expedition and I'll go. It may seem like a lot of money, but it could be worth it to you."

"Perhaps it *would* be worth it," she said thoughtfully. "To see the last of you."

Her eyes were fixed on him with a peculiar intentness, and I noticed the uneasy expression that passed over Pier's face.

21

I could hear the astonishment in my agent's voice.

"What do you mean, you don't know if you should meet with him?" Maury asked. His phone voice was naturally velvety, but now it came as close to a bark as it ever had. "Listen, Carl, these are hard times. Work is work. and Tim Kellogg is talking serious money."

"Yeah, I know, Maury, but . . ." I paused, wondering how I could express it. I knew that my hesitation seemed incomprehensible to him. A few months before, I had been desperately eager to land this job—the very same job that was now available to me again. But things had changed since then.

"I don't know if this is the right time," I said.

I explained to him about my work-in-progress, how I felt I was on the verge of pulling off something big; a fascinating story that I was to some extent living even as I was writing it. All of my time was committed to it, I was totally absorbed, and I didn't feel I should be distracted by mere hack work, no matter how much money was involved.

But none of this came as news to Maury. I had mentioned my book to him before, of course; but he also seemed to know about my relationship with Mirella. Evidently, he had learned about it elsewhere.

When I was through with my explanation, he asked no questions about my novel—or about my personal life. He simply said, wearily but firmly, "Do me a favor, Carl, and show up for this meeting. Just listen to what Kellogg has to say. You might do yourself some good."

And so, to pacify my agent more than anything else, I went once again to the Helmsley Palace to have drinks with Tim Kellogg.

The baby mogul looked even younger than when I had last seen him. In his blue blazer and white sneakers, he might have been a prep school student who was trying to brazen his way into being allowed a drink in the cocktail lounge. The only giveaway of his relative maturity was the scantness of hair that he had combed forward into bangs.

Tim Kellogg was suitably contrite about having originally hired another writer in preference to me—the with-it young rock critic. "It didn't work out," he said sadly. "The boy has talent. But the script he came up with was a mess. No story," he added.

"Does that matter to you?" I asked. I couldn't resist throwing his own words back at him. "I thought you were nonlinear."

"Sure, I'm nonlinear," he insisted. "But a movie has got to have a beginning, a middle, and an end."

We talked story for a while. The tale of the tragic rock star had been fleshed out considerably, now that it had had a go-around in script form. The details of the hero's personal breakdown and career downfall were specified, and some of the notions—I didn't know whether they had originated with Tim Kellogg or with the failed first writer—intrigued me. My story imagination went to work, almost in spite of itself, reshaping what was given, inventing new incidents. Kellogg reacted with enthusiasm each time I came up with a fresh inspiration.

This was turning out to be a productive story conference. And I was beginning to realize that I might have been too inflexible. Big money was at stake; money that could solve my problems, change the course of my life. If all the options on the deal were picked up, and the movie was actually made, it would probably mean a total payment in six figures. I couldn't be cavalier about it, not if all it meant was setting aside two hours every day to work on this project. I wouldn't have to stop work on my novel completely. I would just be slowed down somewhat.

When we came to a pause in our brainstorming, Kellogg sat back and said, "Well, now we're getting somewhere."

"Yeah, I think so," I said.

"I like working with you," he said. "I *want* to work with you."

"Fine. When would I start?"

172

"Right away. If we can do this deal quickly, we'll send you out to the Coast next week."

"The Coast?" I hadn't counted on this. "Why can't I write the script here? Why do I have to go out there?"

"Because I'll be out there. And the director is out there. Filmmaking is a collaborative process, Carl. You can't just phone it in."

"No, I guess not," I agreed uneasily.

"It won't be such a bad life, you know. We'll put you up in a fancy apartment. Provide you with a car."

"How long would I have to be there?"

"Depends on how the work goes. Figure three to six months."

I thought of Mirella, I thought of my book, and I knew that there was no reason to go on with this conversation.

"Sorry, Tim," I said. "I can't do it."

"What?" He looked startled. Then his expression turned shrewd. "Oh, I see. You've got another deal?"

It seemed simplest to let him believe it. "That's right."

"Maury didn't tell me that." He thought for a moment. "Whatever the offer is, I'll top it."

"It's too late for that."

"You're locked in?"

"Locked in."

He shrugged helplessly and went silent.

"Keep me in mind for other things, though," I said.

"Sure, Carl," Tim Kellogg said, unboyish now, his eyes suddenly dead. "I'll do that."

He signaled for the check.

Afterward, I was disturbed. I wasn't bothered so much by what I had sacrificed as by the fact I had sacrificed it for a lie—or at least what was temporarily a lie.

I had talked a brave game with Maury, bragging about my "big book." But the truth was I hadn't been working on my novel at all. I hadn't touched it in two weeks.

It was as if I were constantly tripping on one of Mirella's drugs. My days had become dreamlike. I hovered around Mirella, bent to her wishes, like something boneless and accommodating. My mind, much of the time, was barely in use, but my senses were exercised to their fullest. We made love compulsively, gluttonously; we made love two and three times a day.

And I was deluding myself if I thought I was learning anything more that I could use in my book. I had acquired circumstantial details about Mirella's present life in the East Eighty-fourth Street house. But I knew no more now about what had happened in Ferrara than when I had talked with Mrs. Walling and Tari. I was no closer to solving the mystery of Tobias Walling's death—if, indeed, there was a mystery.

My meeting with Tim Kellogg, if nothing else, had served one good purpose. It reminded me that I was a professional, with a professional's obligations. I decided that it was time to tell Mirella that I would be seeing her less, that my work would have priority again.

I had met with Kellogg at the end of the afternoon. I hadn't known how long it would go on, so I had made no dinner arrangements with Mirella, telling her I would drop by later in the evening, around nine.

When I arrived at the house, I found her in an edgy state. "Let's not stay here," she said, almost at once. "Let's go out somewhere."

"Out? Where?"

"We could go to a movie. Is there any movie you want to see?"

"We can walk up to Eighty-sixth Street and see what's playing," I said.

I wasn't averse to taking in a late movie. But it was puzzling that Mirella would propose the idea. She wasn't a movie fan.

"Is there something the matter?" I asked.

"Piers called," she said, her face darkening. "We had an unpleasant conversation."

"Yeah? Okay, but why do we have to leave the house?"

"He's coming here. I told him he shouldn't, but he insisted. I don't want to be here when he arrives."

I didn't ask about the specifics of their argument. But evidently it had been a serious one, and I didn't want to be there either, if there was any likelihood in might continue.

"Let's go," I said.

We left the house and started walking down East Eighty-fourth Street, a quiet, tree-lined street of brownstones. It was a warm night. The humidity was enervating, and we walked at an easy pace. Now that we were away from the house, Mirella was relaxed again.

After we had gone a half block, I brought up what was on my mind. "I've been screwing off too much lately," I said. "I'm going to have to get back to work."

Mirella glanced up at me and, with a teasing smile, asked, "Have I been distracting you, darling?"

"That's putting it mildly."

After a moment she asked, "What *is* this book you are writing?" It was the first time she had ever inquired about it.

"Just a novel."

"Is it like your last one?"

"Better, I think."

"I would like to see it some time," she said.

"Well," I said vaguely, "maybe you will."

We had crossed York Avenue. Up ahead near First Avenue, on our side of the street, something was happening—or had happened. Two police cars had just pulled up. Cops were getting out of the squad cars and hurrying over to the front of a brownstone. A crowd had gathered on the sidewalk.

Mirella stopped. She seemed suddenly apprehensive. "Let's cross the street," she said.

She wanted to avoid street ugliness, I assumed. But I had an unfailing curiosity when it came to dramatic New York scenes. "No," I said, "I want to see what's going on."

I took her arm and walked on. Mirella didn't resist, but her face was tense and she said nothing as we approached the crowd.

The crowd had formed in a half circle. It consisted of fifteen or sixteen people, all of whom were looking at something that was within the small, sunken front yard of the brownstone. From the somber expressions on their faces, I could tell that whatever it was, it was an unsettling sight.

The front yard was surrounded by a low, cast-iron fence. It contained some bushes, a couple of garbage cans, and, as I saw when we joined the crowd, the still figure of a man, lying on his back at the bottom of the three stone steps. A paramedic was bending over him, blocking my view of his face. But I could see that a bloodstain was spreading on the front of his short-sleeved white sports shirt and that his pockets were turned inside out, as if a mugger had gone through them quickly. The paramedic was searching for signs of life. There didn't seem to be any.

The paramedic straightened up to say something to the policemen who were standing beside him. And now I saw the face of the dead man.

"Oh, my God!" I said, with shock.

It was Piers Allison.

I heard a sharp intake of breath beside me, as Mirella recognized him, too. I was about to put a steadying arm around her. But I was stopped for a moment by the sight of a man standing near the iron fence, who had turned and was staring at us.

A big man in a seersucker suit, with close-cropped gray hair, he was focusing on us intently, with seeming recognition. I had had an initial impulse to step forward and identify ourselves to the policemen as friends of Piers. But, with this man studying us, I changed my mind. I simply returned his stare uneasily.

I looked at Mirella now. She was gazing at Piers's body impassively. She seemed unshaken by the sight; she showed no grief. Her eyes held only the accepting calm of someone who has seen a problem reach its inevitable solution.

"We can go home now," she said.

22

I didn't spend the night with Mirella. I was too shaken and confused, and suddenly found her presence unsettling. I couldn't get the image out of my mind—the look on her face as she gazed at Piers Allison's bloody corpse.

She had been conventionally sorrowful after we got back to the house. She had expressed sadness at the loss of her dear friend, horror at what had happened to him. but these came across as hollow sentiments. Her true response, I suspected, had been revealed in her initial reaction to the sight of Piers's body. Cold-blooded and emotionless. Satisfied.

Near midnight, when I returned to my apartment, I sat in my living room and slowly downed a glass of straight scotch, trying to calm my nerves. And I pondered Piers Allison's violent end, trying to make sense of it.

On the surface, it had been one of the most banal of New York nightmares—a mugging murder. The papers were full of them. Piers himself had expressed his fear of just such a thing happening to him when, only half jokingly, he had said he was "wondering which one of your crazed welfare cases is going to cut my throat." Finally, he had been confronted by the actuality of it. He had had an adventurer's instincts, and he probably wouldn't have reacted in the sensible way of the domesticated New Yorker, passively submitting. He would have resisted, thus inviting the blade that had plunged into his heart.

This all seemed very plausible. But I was bothered by a nagging thought, an idea that wouldn't have occurred in a normal person's mind, but that sprung up readily in my fiction writer's imagination.

Wilfredo—or one of his associates—could have committed the murder, could have carried out the crime at the behest of the mistress to whom he was devoted. This wasn't such a farfetched thesis, and it could be supported by three facts. Mirella had known that Piers was coming over to her house. She had been very nervous. Uncharacteristically, she had wanted to get away from the immediate neighborhood.

Also—and I kept returning to this—there was her chilling reaction when we had come upon Piers's body, a reaction that showed no surprise at all.

Of course, I reminded myself, this might have been the stoic acceptance of a woman whose life had already been affected by murder and sudden, unexpected death. Piers might simply have fitted into a tragic pattern she knew all too well.

Still, she had a motive for murder, if what Mrs. Walling and Tari supposed was actually true—that Piers had been blackmailing Mirella. If the blackmail had been a reality, then Mirella was probably responsible for Tobias Walling's death. If she had killed Tobias, couldn't she just as easily have killed Piers, too?

I stopped myself there. I had long ago decided that Mirella was innocent of Tobias's death, and here I was suddenly envisioning her as a mass murderer. I was becoming as paranoid as all the others.

I went to bed and tried to blank out my mind. But the dark thoughts wouldn't recede. It was a long time before I fell asleep.

In the morning I went directly to my typewriter. It took me a few minutes to warm up, but then the story seized me again and soon I had my full writing momentum going.

At eleven the phone rang. A bit annoyed by the interruption, I went out to the living room and picked up the receiver.

"Hello?"

"Carl?" It was Denny. "How are you?"

She had asked the standard question with real concern, as if she thought there was a possibility I might be ill or otherwise in trouble.

"I'm fine," I replied. "Working."

I felt constrained with her. After I had returned to Mirella, I had stopped seeing Denny completely. I hadn't offered much in the way of explanation. The one time she had called, I had simply informed her of the resumption of my relationship with Mirella, and let it go at that.

"I want to get together with you and have a talk," Denny said. Her tone was very serious and her words came a little stiffly, as if she was reciting a speech she had rehearsed. "It's important, I think. We have to clear up some things between us."

She was insisting on an explanation after all, it seemed, and I had to admit I owed her one. "All right. When?"

"Today, if possible."

"Well, I'm working straight through until dinner," I said. "What are you doing for dinner?"

"I'm having dinner out with some people. But it shouldn't take long. I can be back at my place by ten."

"Should I stop by a little after ten?"

"Yes," she said. "I'll see you then."

Denny lived only a couple of blocks away from the spot where Piers Allison had been murdered. I thought of this as I arrived in front of her building. Her brownstone was on the same kind of street we had walked the night before, tree-lined and seemingly tranquil. It was one of the so-called safe blocks, but now I looked uneasily both ways, as if Piers's knife-wielding killer might still be in the vicinity.

I went up the steps and rang Denny's doorbell, the bell for the top-floor apartment. I was prepared to announce myself over the intercom, but Denny simply buzzed me in. I was struck—more so now than I would have been previously—by how unwise this was; in New York, you never take for granted that someone friendly is coming up the stairs. But Denny, I knew, was the trusting, pure-hearted type who found it inconceivable that anyone would ever do harm to *her*.

She was waiting on the top landing, solemn-faced as she greeted me and rather formal—for a moment, I thought she might actually shake hands. She led me into her apartment and immediately busied herself pouring the coffee she had just prepared.

When we were settled down, cups in hand, Denny said, "I suppose you're wondering why I called."

"You told me. You said you wanted to talk with me."

"Yes—but I would never interfere in your private business. Not on my own, I wouldn't."

I was unsure what she meant by this. "Someone else is involved?"

She was silent for a moment. Then she said, "Maury phoned me. He's worried about you. He asked me to talk to you."

"Why is he worried about me?"

"He thinks you're going to pieces."

"Going to pieces!" I laughed. "That's awfully melodramatic for an agent."

"Well, he's concerned. He says he's concerned about your sanity."

"I bet he is! I just turned down a big movie deal—so, of course, in *his* eyes, that makes me a complete looney. It would never occur to him it might mean I'm tasteful."

"Don't ridicule Maury," she said gently. "He cares for you."

"Well, I care for him," I said. "But he's misunderstanding the situation."

"Is he? He told me something about that movie deal. I don't really understand those things, but I know what the money would have meant for you. Wouldn't it have solved your problem with Nadine? You would have gotten her off your back once and for all."

"Yeah, I suppose so. But I'll make money anyway—from the book I'm writing."

Denny looked uncomfortable at the mention of the book. It was as if she had a thought about it, but was hesitant to voice it. Finally, she did. "Maury doesn't think you're really working on that book."

I stared at her, astonished by the statement. "How can he know? Has he been in my study to see for himself? I have a stack of paper this high on my desk," I said, holding my hand over an imaginary manuscript. "What gives him the idea I haven't been working?"

"He's been hearing things," she said. "He's been hearing that— this is the way *he* put it—you've been spending all your time screwing with some Italian woman." Wryly, she added, "I wasn't in a position to tell him he was misinformed."

"All right, maybe I was goofing off a little. But I got back to work today."

"And it's going well?"

I was about to answer with the automatic positive response—"Terrific!" or some other upbeat term. But, as I met Denny's direct, sympathetic gaze, I lost my impulse to fake it.

"I don't know," I said. "I'm confused."

She looked at me questioningly. "What you were talking about before?" she asked. "Using your real life in a novel? Debasing yourself publicly? That kind of thing?"

I had almost forgotten that philosophical conversation with her. Those concerns still existed, of course. But now the issue had become even more complex, had developed still further nuances.

"Yeah," I said, "but it's gone beyond that." I hesitated, then decided that I might as well tell her. "A man was killed last night. Just two blocks from here."

She looked startled. "What? Who was he?"

"Someone who was part of the real-life story. He was"—I was about to say "a friend of," but then I amended it—"very close to Mirella."

"Who killed him?"

"A mugger. Or it looks like a mugger did it, anyway. But maybe," I said, "he was killed for some other reason. I don't know." The image of Piers, as I had last seen him, came into focus in my mind, almost as sharp and gruesome as it had been in reality. "We saw him."

"Who did?"

"Mirella and I. We saw this man lying in front of a brownstone, near the garbage cans, with all his blood pouring out of him. I've never seen anyone I knew dead before. I mean, dead in coffins, yes—but not dead like *that.*"

"That must have been horrible!" Denny said, her face transformed with empathetic distress. "If you cared for this man."

"I *didn't* care for him—not particularly. But, as I told you, he was part of the story—the one I'm building my novel around." I paused, searching for words that might pin down the vague uneasiness that was at work within me. "I guess what I'm trying to say is, death is much bigger than any book. What I'm doing seemed a little shameful before. Now, with real blood on the pavement—real death—it seems obscene."

After a moment she asked, "But you're going on with your book?"

"Yes."

"And you're continuing your affair with Mirella?"

"For the time being."

"I think Maury is right," she said quietly. "You *are* destroying yourself."

"That remains to be seen."

We had seemingly reached an impasse and were silent for a few moments. Denny put down her coffee cup and retreated into her thoughts. I sat back and took a swallow of the coffee that, up until then, I had barely tasted. In the next building a phonograph was being played loudly and rock music was sifting through the wall. I had been so caught up in what I was saying that I hadn't even noticed it.

At length Denny said, "Maury hopes I can reach you. He feels you might listen to me." She paused. "Would you?"

"I'm listening."

"All right, then," she said. "I don't like the position you've put me in." She was talking in her cool, business voice, which was very calm and pitched a couple of notes lower than her usual tone. "It's not doing either of us any good—to have me playing this role, the nice kid you can come back to whenever things get too ugly with your lady friend."

Her gaze was steady on me and I sensed the resentment in it. Uncomfortably, I asked, "What are you telling me?"

"I'm spelling out the situation for you, as clearly as I can."

"All right. Go on."

"First of all," she said, "I love you. You know that, don't you?"

"Yes."

"I've always imagined we'd get married someday." She looked at me rather insecurely now. "Is that a dumb thing to say?"

"No," I said. "I sort of thought we would, too."

"Well, you can't count on me now," she said. "Not if this goes on any longer. I'm not waiting. It's just too demeaning to me."

"I can understand your feelings," I said. "So, what do you want to do?"

"It's not up to me to do anything. It's *your* decision, Carl. If you break off with this woman right now—break with her completely—then we can go back to where we were. If you don't, I'll never see you again. It will be over between us. That's not an idle threat," she added quietly. "I mean it."

I didn't doubt her. Denny, I knew, had a child's sense of the sanctity of promises and vows. Even if it meant permanent unhappiness for both of us, she would stick by her word.

"I can't make that decision now," I said.

"Then it's finished."

"Don't do that, Denny. Don't kill it. Give me some time."

Her expression turned uncertain. "How much time?"

"A month."

The time period had no special meaning. It was simply the longest delay I thought I could win from her.

"All right," she said. She wasn't such a tough negotiator after all. "But in a month I want your answer."

I finished my coffee and got ready to leave. The basic awkwardness of the situation hadn't been dispelled, and so it was time to go.

Denny accompanied me down the stairs. She stepped out the door with me and stood beside me on the front stoop.

It was physically the closest we had been to each other that evening. I looked into her eyes—eyes that were direct and caring, that had no guile in them—and all the tender feelings I had ever had for her came back to me in a surge.

"No matter what," I said, "I don't want to lose you."

We kissed. It was gentle but sustained; we clung to each other for several moments, banishing the constraint of the last half hour, restoring touch with each other.

When we separated, I glanced down the street. Then I froze.

A woman was standing at the bottom of the stairs, staring up at us. She was an older woman, with gray-black hair drawn tight along the sides of her head. She was wearing—even though the night was still warm—a long, black, capelike coat, and all I could really see of her was her face. It was artificially white, as if a chalky powder was on it. Her mouth was smeared red and her eyes were wild with anger. They were Mirella's dark, burning eyes.

I must have overreacted to the sight of her, because Denny asked in a soft, puzzled voice, "What, Carl? What is it?"

I didn't answer. I kept my eyes fixed on the woman, hypnotized by her mad gaze.

She extended her right hand, with the middle three fingers bent, and made a clawing gesture at us. Then she turned and hurried away down the sidewalk.

23

Raymond flung the half-drained glass of wine away from him. It smashed against the marble of the fireplace.

His head was swimming and he thought he might fall. He looked around desperately to see if there was anyone nearby who could help him. But he was still alone in the room. Isabella had not returned.

There seemed to be no air left around him now. He sucked in deep breaths, but the sense of suffocation welled up in him. He felt starved for oxygen.

Raymond staggered out of the room, heading for the fresh air of the courtyard. As he lurched down the long passageway, his pulse beat pounded insistently in his ears and the stone tilted unsteadily under his feet. He felt the last of his strength leaving him and, in panic, he realized he wouldn't be able to reach the double doors that led to the courtyard.

He was approaching a window that opened out onto a corner of the courtyard. It was closed. He flung himself at it and struggled to open it. If he could get the window raised just a few inches, he thought, the fresh night air would rush in and restore him.

Suddenly, a woman appeared on the other side of the glass. It was the Marchesa. Her face was only a foot away from his and her eyes were staring wildly.

Raymond froze, transfixed by her gaze.

The Marchesa raised her hand, with the middle three fingers bent, as if to claw at him through the glass.

he recoiled from her hand. Then everything blurred—the hand, the Marchesa's pale face—and he felt himself falling, falling back from the window, falling into unconsciousness.

I took the page out of the typewriter, sat back, and read over the section I had just completed. It worked, I decided; it had the effect I intended. It built the narrative to a frightening climax, and yet it answered no questions.

By that point in the story, Raymond had come to suspect that he was being slowly poisoned. But the reader was to be left with several possible interpretations of this scene. Raymond's reaction to the wine he had just drunk might have been the poison at work. And then again it might have been a psychosomatic reaction, the product of his fears and imaginings.

When he tried to open the window and the Marchesa appeared on the other side of the glass, the clawing extension of her hand might very well have been the menacing gesture he took it to be. But there was a more ordinary and undramatic explanation for it, too. She might simply have been reaching out to help him with the window.

There was also a third possibility. The Marchesa might not have been there at all; Raymond, in his delirium, could have been hallucinating.

Ambiguity—the novelist's bread and butter.

Life could be ambiguous, too, I thought, as my mind wandered from my book to what had happened the night before. However, I wasn't as far gone as my fictional protagonist. Raymond may have been subject to visions, but I didn't doubt the reality of what I had seen. There actually *had* been a woman on the sidewalk at the bottom of the stairs. She had watched as Denny and I had kissed. And there had been no mistaking the insane rage on her face.

But who was she? I felt I knew. I couldn't be sure of it on any logical basis. But the sight of her had struck me with the shock of recognition.

I hadn't seen the Contessa clearly that time I had talked with her in the dark. But the face of the woman on the sidewalk was the face I had imagined for her—a strong-boned face that once had had commanding beauty, then had been ravaged by sorrows, with eyes that were large, hypnotic, dark, fathomless—Mirella's eyes, but without coherent thought in them, with madness alive in them.

All right, then, what if it had been the Contessa? What if it was indeed Mirella's mother who had happened upon us, in the course of one of her nocturnal walks? What had aroused such fury in her? The sight of her daughter's lover being affectionate with another woman? It seemed a small provocation for the violent emotion she had shown.

No, I speculated, it might not have had, strictly speaking, anything to do with me at all. Perhaps I wasn't the man she had seen on that stoop with Denny. She might have been seeing someone else—someone gone from the world, but who went on living for her. The faithless Gianfranco.

And now I realized what had chilled me in her look. I had seen murder in her eyes.

That night I didn't stay long with Mirella. When we were through with our lovemaking, I dressed quickly and left the house. I wanted to get home so I could put in another session of work before going to sleep.

I usually walked along East Eighty-fourth Street on my way to the subway, but this time I turned up York Avenue. I didn't want to pass the spot where Piers Allison had been killed.

It was only when I turned the corner that I became fully aware of the footsteps behind me. I had been vaguely conscious of them on Eighty-fourth Street, but merely as an ordinary street sound, the footsteps of a fellow pedestrian. Now that I was walking up York Avenue, I realized that the person had turned the corner also and, quite possibly, was following me.

The footsteps quickened. I glanced back over my shoulder just as my pursuer was catching up with me.

It was the gray-haired man in the seersucker suit, the man who had been in the crowd at the scene of Piers Allison's murder, who had curiously gazed at Mirella and me. He didn't look at me now, but simply fell in step beside me.

After we had walked on about ten yards together, I asked, "Who are you?"

"My name is Dunbar," he answered.

"What do you want?"

187

He turned his head and looked at me. His eyes were watery blue and pink-rimmed. "Mrs. Walling is impatient," he said.

I was momentarily puzzled at the mention of the name. Then the realization came to me. "Oh," I said, "you're the private detective."

Dunbar didn't confirm or deny it. He turned his head forward and walked on beside me in silence.

At length I said, "I didn't promise Mrs. Walling anything."

"You're seeing Miss Ludovisi again," Dunbar said.

"Yeah, but not because Mrs. Walling asked me to. It so happens I enjoy Mirella's company."

He said nothing for a moment. Then he asked, "Have you found out anything?"

"To help you build your case against her, you mean?"

"Anything. Anything that can be useful."

"Not a thing," I replied.

He glanced at me. It was a quick, sharp look, and it told me he didn't believe me.

"Anyway," I went on, "if I *had* found out something, I'm not sure I'd tell you. Why should I do your work for you?"

"This is serious business, Mr. Hopkins," Dunbar said. "There was a death the other night. There could be others."

"What do you mean by that?"

"Mrs. Walling is determined to have justice. Remember that," he said. "She is a very determined lady."

Suddenly, Dunbar was gone. He had abruptly turned down a cross street. I stopped and watched for a moment, as his broad-shouldered figure diminished and turned shadowy.

I was confused now. Had Dunbar meant that last comment as a warning? Or a threat?

And why, I wondered, had he been present at the scene of Piers Allison's murder? If Mrs. Walling's theory was correct, Piers had been Mirella's accomplice, the one who had supplied her with the poison. Was it just a coincidence, then, that Dunbar had been there in the crowd?

There was more than one way to find justice, it occurred to me, to exact retribution.

It was only a thought; I couldn't go so far as to actually suspect Ann Walling of such bloody intentions. She was a proper New England lady, after all, who lived within a strict moral code.

But, as I had come to realize, there were codes at work around me that I didn't fully understand.

I started spending less time with Mirella. I cut short my stays with her. Then I begged off for a couple of evenings in a row. My work, I told her; I had to finish my book.

It wasn't long before she complained—charmingly—that I was neglecting her. "You can't work *all* the time," she said.

"No," I said, "I eat sometimes. And I sleep a little."

"And you play with your mistress," she said.

"What mistress?"

"Your Village mistress. I am your uptown lady. You must have a downtown lady, too."

"My only mistress down there is my book," I insisted. "Believe me."

"Very well, then," Mirella said after a moment, "if you can't tear yourself away from your book long enough to come visit me, I will visit you." With an expression of mock awe, she added, "I have always wanted to see where the great writer does his important work."

At an earlier time, I would have been pleased by her show of interest. But now it seemed a bothersome interruption.

Still, there was no getting out of it. And so, the next evening, I picked her up in a taxi and took her down to Alfredo's on Hudson Street. We dined on veal and pasta and afterward walked over to my building on Abingdon Square.

Mirella made a fuss over my apartment, as if she were taking in some prize-winning interior, rather than an ordinary four-room apartment which, despite my hasty, last-minute efforts, wasn't as clean as it should have been. She admired the views from my windows. She professed delight at my stabs at decor—the Japanese prints and Abstract Expressionist posters. With some interest, she studied my published books, which were standing in a row on the mantle. Once again she vowed to read my earlier novels.

Then she asked to see where I worked. I led her into my study, though there was nothing much in it to show her; it was as bare as a writer's workroom could be.

"Where is the famous book?" she asked.

I pointed to the closed ream box on my desk. Just before leaving that evening, I had taken the precaution of placing my manuscript in the box.

"I put it away when I'm not working on it," I lied.

We went back into the living room. I poured glasses of the Chablis I had bought for the occasion and put my Sinatra records on the record player. It wasn't that I thought it likely that Mirella would be partial to Sinatra. It was just part of my standard operating procedure when entertaining a lady in my apartment.

Actually, corny romantic atmosphere didn't seem inappropriate. Now that I had her in my familiar, everyday surroundings, I was seeing Mirella, almost for the first time, not as an exotic personage, the embodiment of a dark mystery, but simply as an attractive young woman, a companion for the evening, a Village date. Put in this new perspective, she seemed in human scale and—aside from her singular good looks—unremarkable.

When at last we went to bed, the sex wasn't kinky, perilous, testing the depth and breadth of our sensuality. It was relaxed and fun, as, more often than not, it had been with her predecessors in that bed. Afterward, Mirella drifted off to sleep, with a slight smile on her lips. I curled up beside her and soon was asleep, too.

In the middle of the night, I awoke. I reached out, with semiconscious lovingness, for Mirella, and became suddenly aware that she was no longer beside me. I rolled over and looked at the phosphorescent hands on the bedside clock. It was two in the morning.

Where could she have gone? I wondered. She wasn't in the bathroom: the door was ajar and the light was out. I listened, but I heard nothing in the rest of the apartment.

Had she dressed and gone home? Perhaps she had become anxious about her mother. Or perhaps, for some reason, she had felt uncomfortable sharing my bed.

I got up, went into the living room, and looked around. Immediately, I saw where Mirella was. The door of my study was closed, but there was light visible in the cracks.

With a sickening shock of realization, I understood what she was doing. I felt anger and apprehension at the same time. My impulse was to rush forward and confront her—and yet I hesitated, dreading that confrontation.

I was standing there naked. I felt suddenly exposed and vulnerable as it was; I thought it best to cover myself before having it out with her. I hurried into the bedroom, put on my robe, came back out again, and crossed to the study.

I opened the door wide and went in.

Mirella was sitting at my desk, bent forward in concentration, with my manuscript before her. She seemed to be most of the way through it.

At the sound of my entering, she whirled around in the swivel chair and faced me. She was nude, but there was nothing soft and sensual about her now; her whole being was taut with anger.

"How can you do this?" she asked. "To my mother? To me?"

"It's only a story," I said.

"And do you *believe* this story of yours? Do you believe these lies you have written?"

"Of course I don't. It's fiction."

"Fiction!" she repeated bitterly. "And yet you use all the things I've told you! You violate my privacy—you betray my trust—"

"I haven't been thinking of it that way. After all, I'm—" I broke off uncomfortably. I was finding it difficult to brazen this out.

With a thin smile, she said, "I know. You're an artist."

"Yes," I said eagerly, grateful for the help she had just given me, even though it had been in sarcasm. "I don't operate on the level of literal truth at all. I may take a few circumstances from real life. But

191

then, using those few circumstances as inspiration, I spin out something totally artificial from my imagination. And it *is* all imaginary. The girl in the book isn't you. The Marchesa isn't your mother."

"And who is this Raymond? Toby or you?"

"Neither," I insisted. "He is a fictional character—just as they all are."

Mirella seemed calmer now. She was gazing at me with cool thoughtfulness. "But people will think this is the truth," she said, "will they not?"

"They'll think it's a novel."

"Those people who know me—my mother, my family—they'll believe you have revealed something about me."

"If they do, it's not my problem."

"No, but it is my problem." A gentle sadness came into her eyes. It was as if she was beyond anger now and could feel only a resigned sorrow. "This is not a very honorable thing you are doing, Carl. To feed off my pain—my tragedy."

I shifted uneasily under her steady gaze and said nothing.

"Don't you care for me?" she asked.

"Yes, I care for you."

"Very much?"

"Very much."

"Then, because you care for me, you will not publish this book."

"I can't do that," I said. "It's my work."

"It's my *life*, Carl."

I looked away. "I can't do it."

Mirella fell silent. We were at an impasse, and I could see no immediate solution of it. But Mirella seemed intensely thoughtful, as if she was trying to find some way out of this ticklish situation for both of us.

"I wish you'd understand," I said finally.

"I understand."

She said it with unexpected calm, quite reasonably, and I allowed myself to hope that the worst might be over. Her initial reaction was understandable, after all; it had been the shock anyone might have felt in the same position. It was possible that now, after a few moments of reflection, she was beginning to see my manuscript in a balanced, objective way, for what it was—a fantasy, designed simply for entertainment, my daily work and nothing more.

"In a way," I said, "I'm glad you know now. I've felt rotten keeping this a secret from you."

"Have you?"

"Yes. And besides," I went on, "it's been frustrating. I mean, I really would like to have had your help on this."

Mirella smiled slightly, with a touch of incredulousness. "My help?"

For a brief moment I recognized the full outrageousness of the notion. But, on the odd chance, I persisted. "With the circumstantial details. You know; Ferrara, the daily life of the people in the palazzo—that sort of thing. I want it to be authentic and I've researched it, but"—I shrugged—"you can only go so far with research."

"I know," she said, nodding. "I don't mean to be critical—"she hesitated delicately "—but the atmosphere in this book is all wrong. It is clear you never have been in Ferrara. Or in a palazzo."

I was stung—I felt she was being a little unfair—but I did my best not to show it. "I'm sure that's true. But it can be solved," I pointed out. "With your help. I mean, if I'm going to do this, I should get it right."

"Yes," she said slowly. "If you insist on doing this, you *should* get it right."

I looked at her uncertainly. Could she actually be agreeing to my suggestion? "Then you'll help me?" I asked.

"Perhaps. But not now. Later. First," she said, "I must go back to Ferrara."

I was surprised. "You're going back? When?"

"In the next week or two."

"I didn't know that."

"A situation has developed," Mirella said vaguely. "A family concern."

She didn't explain further, and I didn't press her. At that point I wasn't even curious about it. I was more concerned about the prospect of delay in the valuable assistance she now seemed ready to offer me.

"I don't know if I can wait," I said. "I'm almost finished with the book. If you'd just answer a few questions—"

"I will, Carl," she said quietly. "But not now. You must wait a little longer. Then I will answer your questions." Her smile was reassuring, meaningful. "I will give you what you need."

24

Things had changed between us, but not in any clear-cut way. On the surface our relationship went on as before. But Mirella was more closed-off with me now, seeming preoccupied much of the time, serious almost always. She was no longer playful, rarely even sexual. In the week after she read my book, I saw her several times, but we made love only once. And, on that occasion, her heart didn't seem to be in it.

I thought she might be upset by her discovery of the nature of the story I was writing. But she didn't refer to it again, and I had the feeling that actually she was disturbed about something else, something that had nothing to do with me.

Nevertheless, I didn't probe; I was too caught up in my own inner turmoil—and this, too, had nothing directly to do with my book. My real uneasiness stemmed from the fact that I had yet to give Denny my answer. She had agreed to let me have a month to make up my mind, to choose between her and Mirella. More than two weeks had gone by since Denny's ultimatum. There wasn't much time left, and I was still confused.

I could be sure of one thing, though. If I procrastinated and made no decision at all, that would be taken by Denny as my answer. I would lose her forever.

This wasn't an idea I could accept lightly. There were times, in fact, when it seemed intolerable.

My current obsession was Mirella; she dominated my thoughts almost to the exclusion of anyone else. Yet, for all the emotional pyrotechnics involved, I never at any time fancied that I felt real love for her.

My feelings for Denny ran deeper; so deep that I was sometimes unaware of them, ready to deny that I even cared for her. And yet a warm bond with her existed, a sense that any part of my life that wasn't shared with her was life diminished. Did I love her? I had never told her so. But perhaps I did.

Whatever I felt for Denny, it was ongoing, lasting. My obsession with Mirella, on the other hand, might well be transitory, a conflagration that would burn itself out in due time—perhaps as long a time as it took to write a book.

It was the way it happened with my fictional characters. I would create people, become intensely fascinated by them, want no companionship but theirs through all the months I worked on a novel. But once I had sent them out into the world I lost interest in them totally, bored by the mere thought of them. If one of my readers, who had just met these people, brought them up, I would grow restless, be tempted to disown my characters, as if they were acquaintances who embarrassed me.

Perhaps when I delivered this new manuscript to my publisher, Mirella too would start to fade. Just as Isabella, the girl in the story, would inevitably lose interest for me, her original in life might pall on me, seem stale, a thing of my imaginative past. Her meaning extracted, her corporeal presence might seem unnecessary.

In which case wouldn't it be tragic if I had sacrificed Denny for her? Discarded my one solid hope of happiness?

Of course, there didn't necessarily have to be such a dire outcome. The problem at that point was mainly one of bad timing. Mirella had promised to help me with my novel, to furnish the authentic details I needed to give life and credibility to my narrative. Beyond that, there was a chance that she might provide answers to the deeper mysteries in her life. As a writer, I was content with my imaginings; I no longer needed the truth. As Mirella's lover, I suspected I would never be completely free of her without it.

But Mirella would tell me nothing until after her trip to Ferrara. She had reiterated her stand when I brought it up again. And I couldn't pin her down on the date of her trip. All she would say was that it would be "very soon." She still hadn't explained her reason for returning home. I gathered that it had something to do with unspecified family business that was in the process of being resolved. When it was, she would leave for Ferrara.

She indicated that her trip would be only for a week or so, which meant that, if she promptly kept her promise on her return, I could still meet my deadline with Denny, give or take a few days. With the core research on my novel done, some mysteries perhaps resolved, I would be free to return to Denny—if that was my choice.

As the days went by without any definite word of Mirella's departure, I grew increasingly nervous. Finally, I decided I had to confront her about it.

At the end of an afternoon, around five, I dropped by her house. When Porfiria let me in, I saw that there was a wetness under her eyes. The maid had been crying. What was the matter with her? I wondered. Had Wilfredo been mean to her?

She told me that her mistress was in the garden and disappeared. I went through to the rear of the house.

Mirella was sitting in a wrought-iron chair, reading a hardcover novel. She looked up at me, greeted me quietly, gestured to an empty chair near her, and went back to her book. It was a synthetic fantasy about glamorous rich ladies who had wild affairs. I sometimes deplored her taste in fiction, but Mirella—a glamorous, rich lady in her own right—had an insatiable appetite for this kind of fare.

I sat and kept my silence. She seemed neither to object to my presence nor to want it in particular. I was serving as company of sorts for her, I supposed, as she read on. She turned the pages steadily.

Then the pages stopped turning. Her eyes hadn't moved from her book, but I realized that her mind had wandered.

At length, she looked up at me. "You want to ask me something," she said.

"Yes."

"What is it?"

"Can you tell me now what day you'll be leaving for Italy?"

"Not yet."

"Why can't you decide?" I asked impatiently.

"I told you. It depends on other factors."

"But haven't these factors been clarified for you at all? Why are you so helpless about it? Why do you have to wait to decide?"

"We have no power over some things," she said quietly. "They are decided for us."

As she finished saying this, Mirella briefly glanced up at the top of the house. It was as if her thought might have some connection with the resident of the darkened top floor.

After a moment I said, "Well you're hanging *me* up."

"Your book, you mean? I'm sorry," she said, with cool indifference.

"It's not just the book. I want to get it out of the way, sure—so I can clear my mind. There's something else," I went on, "a decision I have to make very soon."

"What decision?"

I paused uneasily. I was aware that I might be about to make the situation worse. But I had come there with the intention of being totally frank with her. And so, after a moment of hesitation, I continued. "I saw Denny not long ago. We had a talk."

"Ah, Denise," she said softly.

I couldn't tell if what I had said was news to her. I suspected that the Contessa had reported to her daughter about my late-night visit to Denny's apartment. But Mirella would have had the same calm expression even if my statement had come to her as a surprise.

"And what did you talk about?" she asked mildly.

"About whether or not we had a future."

"Denise and you?"

"Yeah. We were very close, you know; still are. We never really discussed it, but I guess we were gradually heading toward marriage."

"What happened?" She looked at me with wide-eyed innocence. "Did *I* interfere?"

"Interfere! You moved into my head and just took over! I wake up to the thought of you—I go to sleep to the thought of you—"

"That's sweet," she murmured. "But I don't suppose Denise appreciates it, does she?"

"Hardly," I said. "She's given me an ultimatum. I have to choose between her and you. If it's you, she says she'll never see me again."

Mirella thought for a moment. Then she shrugged. "Well, that's your choice," she said. "I'm not competing for you."

"I know that. You're too proud. Anyway," I went on, "why should I mean that much to you? You can have any man you want."

"Perhaps. But I do want *you,* Carl."

"Fine—but for what? This day-to-day thing we have? It won't last forever."

"I think of the future, too. I'm like any healthy American girl. I want a husband, a family."

This stopped me for a moment. I somehow had never thought of Mirella in this domestic context—or imagined myself in such a picture with her.

"You've never talked about it," I said.

"No," she said. "It's too soon after Toby."

I understood her emotional delicacy about it. But I also understood that this talk of vague future possibilities wasn't solving my present problem.

"Well, I still have to make up my mind about this," I said.

"Yes, you do."

Mirella was regarding me very coolly, and now I realized how mistaken I had been. I had thought that I could be candid with her, talk to her as a friend—in much the same way that I might have discussed Mirella with Denny. But there was no empathy in her eyes. Rather than eliciting her understanding, I sensed that I had awakened the hard, alien thing that was at the core of her.

"You must make your decision soon," she said. She paused. "Otherwise, it might be made for you."

I didn't stay on. When I left, we made no plans to see each other the next day. The next morning and afternoon went by and she didn't even phone me. It was a little unusual to have no contact with her at all in a twenty-four-hour period. I assumed she was leaving me alone, allowing me to work out my problem without distraction from her.

When evening came, I prepared a light dinner for myself and afterward sat at the table, lingering over my coffee, as I thought over my dilemma once again.

My conversation with Mirella hadn't dispelled any of my confusion. If anything, it had increased it. Because a new factor had been added—not an important one, perhaps, but an intriguing one.

Mirella had suggested that she hoped to marry me eventually. It was a possibility I hadn't ever considered. When the Contessa told me that I was destined to be "the man in the family," I thought she meant that I was to be a permanent lover-companion—as poor Gianfranco had been. It hadn't occurred to me that I might take the place of the late Count Ludovisi as the head of the family.

It was a preposterous idea, of course. But the romantic in me warmed to the notion. I briefly entertained an image of myself as the master of the palazzo, sleek and aristocratic, tending to centuries-old rituals of elegance. If nothing else, it would be as far away as I could get from my struggling Greenwich Village self, the confined and grubby peddler of stories that I presently was.

And there would be money. Millions and millions of dollars. A less scrupulous man than I would have jumped at the opportunity for the sake of that alone.

Was I scrupulous? I wondered. Or was I just dumb? Certainly this deserved longer thought.

No, I reminded myself, Mirella wasn't a real person. She existed for the sake of my novel. In the normal course of things, she would cease to exist for me when I had written the last page of my novel. If I married her, I would risk crossing over into my created fiction, becoming one with it; I might lock myself into my own fantasy.

The phone rang. I rose, went over to it, and picked up the receiver. "Hello?"

"Oh, Carl! Thank God, you're there!" It was Denny and her voice was breathless.

"Denny, what's the matter?"

"I don't want to be alone. Please, Carl, come up here! Something's happened—and I can't be alone!"

"What happened?"

There was a brief silence. Then she said, "I was nearly killed."

"When? How?" I asked quickly.

"When I was on my way home from work. A car almost hit me."

"An accident?"

"Maybe. I don't know." The urgency came back into her voice. "I'm frightened, Carl. Please, come be with me!"

"I'll be right there."

In the cab going uptown, I tried to understand what might have happened—but I could only guess at it. Near brushes with death in New York traffic were commonplace occurrences. And yet this seemed to have been something more than that. There had been real terror in Denny's voice.

This time, when I rang Denny's bell, she called down through the intercom. "Carl?"

"Yeah, honey," I said into the speaker. "It's all right, it's me."

She buzzed me in and I ran up the flights of stairs to her apartment. Denny was waiting for me in her doorway. She still had on the blouse and skirt that, doubtless, she had worn that day at work.

She put her arms around me, buried her head on my shoulder, and held me tight for a few seconds in a wordless embrace. It was as if the physical comfort of me was all that she needed.

Then she stepped back and we went into her apartment. "Maybe I didn't need to make you come up here," Denny said with an apologetic little smile. "I'm feeling better now."

She settled onto the couch and I sat opposite. As I studied her, I wasn't sure she actually had recovered from whatever fear had seized her. She looked pale and tense, and there was an abiding anxiety in her eyes.

"Okay," I said. "Tell me exactly what happened."

"An accident," she said. "That's what I keep telling myself. It was just an accident." Her expression clouded with uncertainty. "But I don't know—he had such a look on his face!"

"Who did?"

"The guy who was driving the car."

"Let's take it from the beginning," I said patiently. "Where did this accident happen?"

"Down at the corner. I had just gotten off the bus. I walked up a block, the way I always do, and then I started to cross the street. This gray car came out of nowhere—like it was lying in wait for me. I felt it bearing down on me from behind, and I whirled around. It was coming straight at me. I jumped out of the way at the very last moment. It shot past me and crashed into a traffic signal. Hit it so hard it broke the pole in half. Then the man in the car jumped out and ran away." This methodical recitation of the details seemed to have calmed her. In a matter-of-fact voice, she concluded, "When the cops came, they checked out the license plate. It was a stolen car."

"You say you saw the driver's expression?"

"Yeah. I got a good look at him when he was coming at me. He was Puerto Rican, and he had a funny, excited smile on his face. I don't know," she went on, "maybe he was just stoned. But it seemed like he was trying to hit me deliberately—and enjoying it."

"How old was he?" I asked.

"In his twenties, I suppose."

"What did he look like?"

"Thin—with a mustache. I can't describe him any better than that."

"How did you know he was Puerto Rican?"

"He looked it. Hispanic, anyway."

"Could he have been Cuban?"

She seemed a little puzzled by my question. But then she answered, "Yes, he could have been Cuban."

I couldn't ask her anything more. I didn't have the will for it. I was too chilled by the horror of what I was now thinking.

Denny was staring at me, reading my expression. A disturbed, apprehensive look came onto her face. "This doesn't have something to do with—?" she began, then broke off.

When I remained silent, she asked in a small, childlike voice, "Is someone trying to hurt me?"

I saw a tremor of fear go through her. I rose, went to her, sat beside her, and put my arm around her.

"No one's trying to hurt you," I said. "It was an accident."

25

I was awake now, out of the dream. As I walked the streets, after leaving Denny's apartment, going in no particular direction, I saw what I had been doing, saw it clearly for the first time in many months. The mists of romantic fiction had lifted. I perceived my actions in bright, everyday colors, recognized my responsibilities as a sensible, moral human being—and as a man who loved and cared for a woman.

I had endangered Denny. Beyond everything else, I could not forgive myself for that. I had brought her within inches of a brutal, senseless death. I winced with anguish every time I imagined it, the lethal mass of steel rushing past her. I berated myself for it. I knew I had only myself to blame.

The face of the madwoman came back to me now, that strange, enraged woman who had looked up at us from the sidewalk, who had reached out to claw at us. I remembered the hate that had twisted her features. I should have realized then that all her malevolence hadn't been directed at me alone. It had threatened Denny, too.

More and more, my thoughts returned to the Contessa. I had come to recognize her as the source of the evil, as the spirit that presided over the acts of violence, the bloodthirsty dark goddess whose wrongs could only be satisfied by death. In her madness the Contessa could cast a powerful spell—over her daughter, and over those, like myself, who had entered too deeply into Mirella's life.

It was time to break the spell, I decided. I couldn't rescue Mirella from it, nor was I inclined to try. But I could terminate my part in her story.

I turned down Eighty-fourth Street and walked rapidly until I was at Mirella's door. When I rang the first time, no one came. I rang again and finally heard footsteps approaching.

It was Mirella herself who opened the door. Her face was solemn and her eyes were so blank that for an instant I thought she might be under the influence of one of her drugs. But then her expression brightened with a smile of gladness at the sight of me. Or it started to, anyway. When she became aware of my grimness, her smile faded.

"I want to talk to you," I said.

Mirella simply nodded and stepped back to let me enter. Then she led me into the living room.

She turned in the center of the room and faced me squarely, as if she was bracing herself for a statement she was already anticipating.

"I'm not going to see you again," I told her.

Her expression didn't change. "You have made your choice?"

"Yes," I said. "I love Denny. I'm going to marry her."

"I see," she said. "Then this is it? Goodbye?"

"Yes. It's goodbye."

She was silent for a moment. Then, with a shrug, she said, "I am not surprised."

"No, I didn't think you'd be."

Mirella gestured for me to sit, with polite formality, as if I were once again an unfamiliar visitor, a stranger. I sat on the couch and she sat opposite me.

There was an unusual stillness in the house, I noticed. It was always quiet, of course, but now the silence was absolute. One light was on in the living room, but it seemed to be just about all the light there was. I had a sense that the darkness had intensified throughout the rest of the house.

At length Mirella asked, "Will you explain your decision? I am curious as to how you arrived at it."

"Finally, it was made simple for me," I replied. "Someone went too far."

"What do you mean?"

"Denny was nearly killed today." I paused. "But perhaps you know that."

"No, I don't know!" Her eyes were wide with astonishment. "What happened?"

I was studying her closely and I was sure her reaction was genuine. The finest actress could not have feigned the startled look in her eyes.

"A car almost hit her," I said.

"Is she all right?"

"Yes, she's all right."

"Oh, good."

I felt a little easier—about Mirella, anyway; though I had never really lost my belief in her innocence. I had originally judged her to be incapable of killing anyone. I had had my moments of doubt since, but now I was convinced of it again.

Mirella was looking at me expectantly, waiting for my explanation, and I continued. "What happened to Denny today may not have been an accident. Someone may have tried to kill her."

She frowned. "Who would do such a thing?"

"I don't know," I said. "It could be someone who wanted to force a choice on me, who wanted to make sure that I stayed with you."

Her expression was suddenly guarded. "What are you talking about?"

There was no turning back now. I had to say it all, no matter how painful it might be for both of us.

"There have been unexplained deaths," I went on. "Piers Allison. And Tobias's death, too. That's never been explained to everyone's satisfaction."

Her eyes were fixed on me. "So?"

"Your mother was there, wasn't she, when Tobias died? You had arranged her escape from the mental institution. And she was still in Italy. You were hiding her in or near Ferrara. Right?"

I didn't know what to expect: an angry denial, an emotional confession, or a total retreat into herself. But Mirella reacted in no way in particular. She was thoughtful for a few moments, as if she was weighing what I had just said, as if she was trying to determine how much I really knew.

"Yes," she said finally. "She was nearby."

"And she had access to the palazzo?" I asked. "To the servants who had always been loyal to her?"

Her calm vanished. "What are you suggesting?" she asked, in a sharp whisper.

"And here, too," I persisted, "she has loyal servants here? Porfiria is devoted to her? Would do anything for her? And Porfiria has Wilfredo to do anything that is asked of him?"

"Are you saying that my mother—" There was pain on her face and she could barely get the words out. "My mother—?"

"Your mother has killed once," I said. "She may have killed more than once."

Mirella let out a stifled cry and put her hand over her eyes.

I felt sick with guilt now. But I reminded myself that I was doing this for Mirella's sake, and went on. "I know this is hard for you to accept. But your mother should be back in the institution. It was wrong of you to take her away from there."

She lowered her hand and stared at me. "You say this to *me?*"

"I'd say it to your mother, too. I'm not afraid of her. I'd confront her with this."

"Very well, then," Mirella said, rising. "You will confront her. Now."

I looked up at her uncertainly. I hadn't expected her to take my statement so literally. I was suddenly apprehensive, as I realized that she was asking me to live up to my words.

But I knew I should go through with it. It would give me a chance to question the Contessa directly about my suspicions. Perhaps then I could bring the situation to a head, make Mirella see what she must do, and end the danger for Denny and myself.

I rose and followed Mirella out of the living room. We ascended the stairway, with Mirella staying a couple of steps ahead of me. We reached the third floor and then went on up the stairs to the top floor.

As we approached the last landing, I saw the flicker of candlelight. It wasn't coming from the front room on the other side of the archway—the room in which I had had my conversation with the Contessa—but, rather, it was illuminating the large rear area that included the landing itself.

Mirella stopped on the top stair and gazed at someone or something in the rear room. I had halted several steps below her and I could see nothing. But I could hear a woman's voice now, muttering a steady flow of incomprehensible words.

Mirella turned back to me and indicated with her head that I should continue to the top. I climbed the last few stairs. She stepped aside to let me pass, but I paused first, turned, and looked.

Porfiria was kneeling at the foot of a bed that was at the center of the nearly bare room. She was praying aloud, with grief-stricken intensity. A woman in a white, brocaded gown was on the bed, propped on the pillows in a half-sitting position, with her eyes closed and her hands folded on her stomach. A crucifix had been inserted into her still, stiff hands.

I crossed and looked down at the dead woman's face. It was gaunt, almost skeletal, with transparent, white skin. It was the face of a drained old lady whose life had seeped slowly from her.

I had never seen this woman before. Her face was unfamiliar. It bore no resemblance to the face in my memory, that of the madwoman who had threatened Denny and me.

I stared at the Contessa for several moments, too numbed by my realization to think any clear thought. Then I became aware that I was no longer hearing Porfiria's voice. I glanced toward the foot of the bed. She was gone.

I turned. Mirella was standing near me.

"When did it happen?" I asked.

"She passed away a few hours ago."

"Had she been ill a long time?"

"For many years. It was cancer," she said. "It was why I took her away from that terrible place. I did not want my mother to die among strangers, as a prisoner. She could only be safe here, with me, in this country. Here she could die in peace, in the company of those who loved her. Porfiria and I were at her side when she died. No one else. It was as it should be."

Mirella gazed at the dead woman. Along with the sorrow on her face, there was a gentleness, a tenderness that I had never seen in her expression before.

"We can go home now," she said. "I will take her back tomorrow evening, to be buried next to my father. My mother will be home at last." She looked at me again. "I will be home, too."

I stood there in silence for a moment, unable to think of what to say. Much had been explained, and yet I was more confused than before.

"Her pain is over now," Mirella said. "She had very great pain. Nothing I gave her could stop it. It crippled her. She hasn't left this bed in weeks." With a thin, bitter smile, she asked, "Is this your monster, Carl? Your dangerous woman who kills people?"

"I'm sorry," I said. "I didn't understand."

"No, you didn't." Her mouth tightened with cold contempt. "You are like everyone else. You need to think evil. You need to see evil."

I was shaken by the rebuke. Still, my mind kept working, struggling to comprehend this. Some questions had been answered. But not all of them.

"I didn't *want* to think that way," I said. "But there were things that couldn't be explained." I paused. "There still are."

I glanced at the woman on the bed, with irrational uneasiness, as if there was a danger she might overhear. But nothing about her suggested even the supernatural chance of it. With her hands folded before her, she was positioned for her eternal rest, and nothing could distract her now.

"You will have her buried?" I asked. "In a family plot?"

"Yes," Mirella said. "Where all the people in my family rest."

"You venerate your dead? Their remains as well as their memories?"

She seemed a little puzzled by the question. "Yes. I do."

"You had Tobias cremated," I said. "Immediately. Why?"

It may have been the swift directness of it. Or it may have been that, standing by her dead mother, she felt constrained from evading, from lying, as she might usually have done. But, whatever the reason, no defenses went into place; she remained naked before my question. There was a resignation in her eyes now, as she met my gaze, a weary awareness, perhaps, that we had gone beyond the point where there could be games and subterfuges.

"The reason is obvious, is it not?" she replied, with a faint, wan smile. "So no one could know the truth."

"The truth," I echoed, fixing the word in place between us, hoping it wouldn't vanish now. "Tell me, Mirella," I asked her gently, "what *is* the truth?"

She didn't answer immediately, but moved away from me to a far corner of the room. I followed her readily, wanting—as perhaps she did also—to put some distance between us and the dead woman on the bed.

At length she turned back to me. "To understand the truth," she said, "you would have to understand Toby. And you did not know him very well, did you?"

"What do you want me to know about him?"

"That he was a weak man."

"We all have our weaknesses," I said.

"I am sure," Mirella said, "and you have learned to live with your weaknesses. But Toby had two special weaknesses that destroyed him in the end." She paused. "One was his little red pills."

"Barbiturates?"

"Yes."

I remembered the bottles of Seconal, hidden in the foot locker at the back of the closet, and I understood now, understood to whom they had belonged. "He was an addict?"

"A terrible addict. He denied it, of course. But he couldn't live without his little red pills. He knew it and I knew it."

After a moment, I asked, "What was his other weakness?"

"A man. A man named Tari."

"Tari?"

Evidently, I had reacted on hearing his name, because Mirella looked at me more intently. "You know him?"

"I've heard him mentioned. Toby and he were close friends, weren't they?"

"More than friends." Her mouth tightened. "Perhaps I should be more tolerant. But I have never been able to understand it. That kind of relationship between men."

What she was suggesting seemed clear enough, but I asked the question anyway. "They were lovers?"

"Toby claimed it was no longer physical—and perhaps he was telling the truth. But he insisted that he had to go on seeing Tari, even after we were married. It didn't seem to matter to him that it would be insulting to me," she said, more forcefully, "a shameful thing! He said that he could never reject Tari"—her voice was tinged with scorn—"that he meant too much to him. He told me this long story about how he had saved Tari's life, and then Tari had saved *his* life."

"When Tobias came back from the hospital?" I asked, remembering Piers Allison's reference to it.

"From Silver Hill, yes. When he was supposed to have been cured of his addiction. Tari took care of him, made sure he stayed off the pills."

"But you say he was taking the pills."

"Yes, he had started again. And he blamed *me* for it. Can you imagine that?" she asked, with a bitter smile. "Blaming me for his own weakness?"

The issue was dead, along with Tobias, but a reflexive anger had come onto her face as she remembered it. I could imagine what fierce arguments had taken place when her wound was new.

"You had fights about that?" I asked. "And about Tari?"

"Tari—and the pills. The last fight was the worst one, when I found the bottle of pills in Toby's suitcase. I made him watch as I flushed them down the toilet. He cried. He said I was humiliating him. He sat down on the floor of the bathroom and cried like a little baby." She lowered here eyes and was silent for a moment. Then, more quietly, she continued. "It was for his own good. But in the end it made no difference. I obviously didn't find *all* the pills."

I just looked at her now, understanding at last what had happened. It was self-evident, plausible, mundane even, and yet, such had been my hunger for dark crime and high drama, it had never really occurred to me.

"He killed himself," I said. "He took an overdose of pills."

She nodded.

"And you had him cremated, so that there wouldn't be an autopsy that would disclose the Seconal in his body. So that no one would know."

"And no one *does* know."

"No. Instead, you're living under a cloud of suspicion. You're allowing people to believe that you have committed a terrible crime."

"It is not nice to live under suspicion," Mirella said. "But it is better than living in shame."

It might have seemed illogical to anyone else, but, after all my months with Mirella, I understood what it meant to her. Always it came down to that: shame. Mirella, like her mother before her, like, for all I knew, the Ludovisi through the centuries, could never confront that— public dishonor, general contempt, the patronizing pity of social inferiors.

It must have seemed a disgrace worse than murder to a woman as proud as Mirella—that the man she had loved had chosen to kill himself rather than go through with his marriage to her. Such a shameful rejection could never be confessed. So she had kept her secret, had endured her guilt alone and in silence, a very different guilt from what I or anyone had imagined.

Suddenly, I thought of my novel. I would have to reconceive it, I realized. I would rely less on the overtly sinister and allow more of the perverseness of human psychology: in particular, the childlike psychology of oversheltered aristocratic women.

Almost unthinkingly, I uttered my thought. "Now I can finish my book."

It was an inappropriate thing to say, perhaps, and Mirella stiffened slightly. "Finish your book?"

"I mean," I went on, "I realize I've had some of it wrong." I felt very uncomfortable, but, having unwisely revealed my thought, I now had to explain it. "I've been concentrating too much on the melodramatic side of things. I haven't fully understood the human motivations involved."

"I have told you this story," Mirella said slowly, "so that you would *not* write this book."

"But it's all right now," I insisted, "don't you see? It really is fiction. Sure, there'll be murders in it. This kind of narrative has to have them. But now I know that none of it has anything to do with real life. It's all stuff I've made up."

Mirella looked at me for a long moment before she spoke again. "There is nothing that can stop you from writing this book, is there?" she said quietly, not as a question, but as if she were accepting it now.

"It's my work." I paused, then gently reminded her, "And you promised to help me, Mirella."

She was thoughtful, then she let out her breath softly, in a sigh of resignation, I assumed—though it seemed almost a regretful sigh.

"Yes, I will help you," she said. "You need the atmosphere of the palazzo, do you not? You need to see it with your own eyes?"

Excitement quickened within me as I guessed what she was about to offer. "It would make all the difference," I said.

"You can come visit me in Ferrara. Tomorrow evening, my mother and I will go back. In two weeks time, you can join me there."

This was more than I had ever dared hope for. I almost laughed aloud at this unexpected stroke of luck. "That would be wonderful!"

Mirella's dark, sad gaze held on me. "You can stay as long as you want, Carl," she said. "All your questions will be answered."

Mirella left two weeks ago tonight. Tomorrow I will depart for Ferrara.

The days that have gone by since the last night I saw her have been fevered for me; I have passed them in a delirium of excitement. I am excited, not simply because I will be able to finish my novel, fleshed-out and accurate in its evocative details, but also because I now recognize that the book has served as a prophetic dream. Like Raymond, the hero of my story, and like Tobias Walling, I have been destined to walk on marble floors, pass under lushly painted ceilings, explore ancient, dark corridors.

And, like all fated heroes, I will be in quest of the elusive truth. Because the remaining questions are more perplexing to me than ever. They have disturbed me waking and sleeping, they have permitted me little rest.

I now accept that my original suspicions were groundless. The helpless, dying Contessa could have had no part in the continuing pattern of violence.

Then who killed Piers Allison? And did someone actually try to kill Denny?

I believe Mirella's story; I believe she was innocent of Tobias Walling's death. I believe it for the same reason I always have—so aristocratic a creature as Mirella, with her exquisite self-regard, would never kill for mere money. But she *is* her mother's daughter, the murderous genes may be within her, and if she did happen to kill it would be for the motivation her mother had—to protect herself from shame.

If Mirella can kill. I am unwilling to accept that. I find it easier to believe in coincidence, that Piers Allison's murder and Denny's brush with death were coincidental happenings.

**For other fine titles from Vivisphere
please visit:**

www.vivisphere.com

or call for a catalogue:

1-800-724-1100